LITTLE WOLF

////

K.T. TOMB

OTHER BOOKS BY K.T. TOMB

The Raccoon King
The Peaches of Wang Mu
The Dagger
Pandora's Box
Tyrannosaurus Knights
Monster
Little Wolf
The Dragon and the Witch
Jerusalem Gold
Curse of the Coins
Ghosts of the Titanic
The Honeymooners
The Tempest
The Swashbucklers
The Kraken
The Last Crusade
Here Be Dragons
Steroid Blues
The Target
The Hunters
The Deal
Kidnapped
Smooth Operator
G-Man

Published by
Quests Unlimited Books

Copyright © 2017 by K.T. Tomb
(Previously published under the pen name, Steve Rollins.)
All rights reserved.

Printed in the United States of America.

ISBN- 9798677290947

LITTLE WOLF

Chapter One

The forest teemed with life.
Sounds of the bluebirds greeting the morning sun rang out through the mountains, echoing across the valley. Mockingbirds and cardinals sang the springtime into being, too. So did the squawking jays and crows. Treetops swayed in the morning breeze. A hushed wind combed through the branches, reaching into the brightening eastern sky. Night creatures spilled forth from the undergrowth, scurrying to their holes and nooks. Cold-blooded creatures slithered into the sun, warming their serpentine bodies enough to hunt.
Then, some of the bigger animals appeared...
A small female wolf returned from the hunt,

a plump quail hanging limply from her jaws. She pushed through ferns and thorny undergrowth, her fur thick enough to withstand most thorns, although some jabbed her flesh. She ignored the pain. She'd suffered through far worse pain than a few embedded thorns.

Once in the cushioned den, matted with pine needles and the fur of long-dead meals, she dropped the fat quail in a far corner. The fowl quivered, staring at her unblinkingly, bleeding from its many wounds. Too broken to fight or run, and too scared to flee, its tiny chest moved rapidly, rapidly, then not at all.

The female wolf looked at it without remorse. It was, after all, only food to her. She must feed… she had a long labor to come and she needed nourishment for the strength to battle through it. Her body quaked with a small tremor as she stepped into the den. She knew the others were still hunting, but the Alpha would return to her in time to stand guard over her labor.

Restless, she paced the small den, her fur brushing free some of the flaking bark of the crisscrossed branches that kept out most of the rain and snow. The den's entrance was small but secure. The ground was warm and soft with the pine straw she'd spent over a week collecting. The fur and feathers of her prey added a soft touch.

She stopped pacing when the hunger within overwhelmed her. Or was it the pain that signaled the impending birth of her cubs? This was her first litter, after all. Finally, she sat before the now-dead quail, and pulled it open with her great jaws and deft use of her paws. She was a wily one, clever and capable.

Later, when her belly was content, she was still anxious. The soon-to-be mother wolf rested her paws on the den's ledge, which led out to the forest. She sensed the life around her and the life that stirred within her womb, too. The pain came quicker now, pulsing through her body. The others were not far from the den; some paused by her den's entrance, staring at her with yellow eyes and often leaving her bits of meat. They knew she would soon be weakened by the whelping.

More tremors. Sharp pains. Her tongue rolled free as she panted and strained. She needed water, but knew she must stay in the den. With eyes closed, she felt the life move within her, and now heard and smelled the Alpha. Such strong footfalls. So confident. So big. His scent, so perfect, rich, and exciting.

Upon his arrival, the Alpha sat quietly outside the entrance to the den and, with him there as guard, she could now focus on the birth of the cubs. She would not eat, drink or sleep until the delivery was complete. Time would stand still for her, as nature took its course.

***

She breathed in deep huffs, her white teeth bared against her curled black lips. She rested on her side in the pine straw and fur and dirt, bracing against the pressure building through her body.

When the first pup dropped, she followed her instinct and nuzzled it, breaking the membranous sac with her teeth and licking it. This bolstered her strength by offering a bit of protein to her body. The blind babe moved slowly across the soft nest, searching for milk. The next pup arrived in a similar ritual, licked clean and pushed toward her already swollen teats. The third arrived, and then a fourth. Mother Wolf looked them over, finding no fault with the pups. Each was marked in its own way. The first had blue-gray markings around the eyes and muzzle. The second had black circles outlining its eyes. The third pup wore a pelt of solid white, which would offer it camouflage in the winter months, and the fourth was solid gray, just like the Alpha.

Now, the Mother Wolf rested her head on

the soft, if not dusty, floor of the den as each pup nursed. She still had energy, but only enough to keep an eye on her young. She noticed that the fourth pup was having trouble finding her milk supply. She nuzzled the babe, licking it to encourage action. She already felt very, very protective over the little ones, so protective that she knew she would fight to the death for them.

Perhaps knowing this, the Alpha moved restlessly outside the den. He sensed the presence of the cubs, but he would not come to her unless she summoned him. She soon would. For now, she relished the company of her new offspring, their small sounds, their small movements. She felt deeply connected to them.

The pack would welcome them soon enough, she knew. Someday, each of them would have caretakers; as such, the entire pack ensured their chance of survival. A collective instinct, perhaps. She and the Alpha had worked hard to build a bonded group, a strong pack, a true family. They hunted well and looked after each other. She loved the idea of her pups growing into strong members of their pack.

Her thoughts were disrupted by the fourth pup falling from her teat and twisting against the straw. His body seized in strange jerking movements, weakness overtaking him. Mother

Wolf pulled him to her with her muzzle and licked him with determination. It was all she knew to do. Shortly, she let out a small sound to alert the Alpha.

His head appeared at the mouth of the den. He seemed to instantly size up the events, and she suspected he'd already had caught the slight change in scents as the pup's condition had taken a turn for the worse. The Alpha found a way through the small space and nuzzled at the little creature. But the little one, she saw now, was unmoving.

Long after the Alpha had retreated, Mother licked at the lifeless babe, his little head resting on the smooth ground. Later, when she stopped licking at the lifeless body, and attended to the cubs who again demanded her attention, Alpha appeared again. He gently picked up the dead pup's small body with his great teeth, and left the den with it.

She had never felt this sense of loss before. It was as if a part of her was gone, a part she would never know again. She had the others, and a lively trio they were, but her maternal instinct was strong for all of her offspring and it was heartbreaking to lose even one of them. After sniffing the ground where the dead pup had lain, the mother turned her attentions back to the remaining three, all of which nursed greedily, so young that they were unaware of their lost brother.

As the realization sank in that she would never know where Alpha buried the dead cub, she became even more distraught. Mourning the loss of the dead cub, she howled softly to herself. It was a song of death and loss and pain.

***

Nestled at the edge of the very same forest was a small blue house, a house where another canine birth was in progress.

The small mother dog curled around her puppies in a cardboard box at the back of the Andersons' garage. The poodle had labored through the night at the same rate and time as her canine cousin who labored deep in the forest. When the sun rose, casting squares of sunlight onto the living room carpet, the people of the house began to rise, too. The coffee pot gurgled to life automatically, sending the scent through the house to awaken the humans of the abode.

"What day is it?" Mrs. Anderson muttered as she drifted into wakefulness.

"Saturday," her husband replied with equal alertness, or lack thereof.

"What is that sound?" she asked.

From beneath their bedroom, in the garage, came a muffled cacophony of newborn yips and muted barks from the mother dog.

Mr. Anderson sat up and rubbed his face. He pulled on the tee shirt that lay on the nightstand next to the bed, swung his feet to the floor and stretched his arms over his head.

"I hear it," he said. "After I've had a cup of coffee, I'll take a look." He stood and shuffled his way to the bathroom.

The woman stood and pulled on her robe. She rubbed her eyes, happy that the weekend had arrived. She had a little work to do, but she could put that off until the afternoon. She would get a cup of coffee and then check in on Bree. Her purebred miniature poodle had gotten sullied by a roaming mongrel and they had been waiting for her to drop the litter. If they could dispose of the pups quietly, they would still be able to present her as a breeding dog. Her bloodline had remained pristine up until the incident. They couldn't take them to the pound as that required an exchange of information and a lie that the mother dog had died. If word got out, their reputation would be ruined.

"Oh, Bree," Mrs. Anderson said after opening the garage door. The expensive plush corduroy dog bed lay untouched. The small white dog curled around her litter on top of the cardboard box housing a pile of old towels. The mother dog raised her head and yipped a greeting to her human. She had whelped two puppies through the night, a small litter, but she felt the surge of maternal pride and hoped her human would accept them into their small family. The puppies climbed over each other, both bearing the short, curled fur of their mother. Mrs. Anderson noticed, however, that the shape of their muzzles and eyes looked different from the diminutive lines of the mother's face. They had more of a sleek visage. It was difficult to know immediately what breed may have fathered them. Bree's tail wagged with happy anticipation of the human's acceptance of her pups.

Mrs. Anderson pulled her robe closed against the morning chill, cupping her hands around her coffee mug as she looked over the small pups next to Bree. She tried to ignore the pang in her heart as she examined them. They were pretty puppies, despite the circumstances of their existence, but she knew that their future wouldn't be pretty. Perhaps she could buy them some time. She heard the door open as Mr. Anderson joined her in the garage.

"She finally popped," he said, taking a swig of his coffee and placed an arm around her shoulders.

"Don't be crass," she said, turning away and shrugging off his arm. Faced with the circumstances, she had no interest in receiving affection from him, regardless of how casual the intent.

"Oh, come on, honey," he said. "You know what has to be done."

"But why?" she cried, turning an accusatory eye toward her husband. "Why do we have to do away with them in such an inhumane way? And look at Bree! She is so happy, look at her tail wagging. It will break her heart to lose them and you know it!"

He rubbed his hand on the back of his neck. "Would you sacrifice everything we've worked for?" he said, pulling the card that he knew would make his wife cave. "All the work we've put in to assure the Club owners that Bree was pedigreed? Would you face the scandal that would follow if they found out she's been compromised? You saw what happened last year with the Gentrys. Do you want that to happen to us?"

"Of course not," she replied. "But look at them, darling. They are so helpless. At least give them a week, so they have a chance of surviving. Can we at least do that?"

He sighed. The pups would remain dependent on nursing during that time. But after they were weaned, would become too active, noisy and too much of a liability. "A week," he said. "No more. We cannot afford for a whisper of question as to why Bree is not in breeding rotation at the right time. Just last week at the meeting, Mr. Joseph had inquired about her well-being. We just can't afford it, honey."

She slumped against his chest, letting his arm drape across her shoulder. "I know," she whispered. "It breaks my heart, but you are right."

At their feet, Bree wagged her tail and peered up at her beloved humans, her heart swelling with pride. Her humans would take care of the puppies just as a wild pack would. She laid her head down to rest after her arduous night, while her two pups nuzzled at her with contented sighs.

***

The mother wolf ran through the forest.

She had left the Alpha to watch after the cubs for a little while, as she had been caring for them for several days and needed to run, to drink, and to privately mourn the cub she had lost. The others in the pack had a connection with her mental state, as she had with theirs and she knew that her continued sadness would eventually weaken them all.

The wind rushed past her as she bounded through the woods, trees rushing by on either side. The others stayed behind, making an informal circle around the den. They had all already hunted for the day and felt content to stay. The exercise bolstered her mood and she knew in her mind connection that the others felt it, too.

She sensed the Alpha pacing the entrance to the den. If she concentrated enough, she would even hear through his ears the sounds of their yips and barks, now stronger than they had been at birth. In the weeks to come, they would be taught how to call to the others—the most important element of wolf communication besides the ever-present mind link.

She ran, though she knew not to stray too close to the forest's edge. There were hunters and the strange creatures that barreled along the hard roadways; large dragon-like beings with bright glowing eyes, which flew level with the ground. They had lost one of theirs in the last season to one of these creatures. Foxfoot had tried to run across the hard road to join them on the other side, but he had been hit quite suddenly by one of those large flying creatures as it came around the edge of the rocky outcropping.

They had mourned Foxfoot and decided not

to approach the hard roads again. It had been many years since they had lost anyone to a hunter at the forest's edge, but she knew of other packs that had lost important members.

She stopped, listening to the sounds of the forest. A squirrel disturbed the brush a little way away from her. She could have given chase if she chose, but she wasn't hungry. The pack had brought her food since the birth of the pups, keeping her strength up during the nursing stage. Soon, she knew her pups would awaken and they would then begin to learn the ways of the wolf. She kept her senses tuned to the actions of the small squirrel for a brief moment, but she decided she needed to return to the den. Her pups needed to nurse soon.

The pack grew restless at her absence, even as the Alpha calmed them. He chastised the pack through the mind link. *Let her be*, he would have said. *She brings you new pack mates and that is to be respected*. They all knew it. Especially, Cass, the female who had positioned herself to be the Alpha's primary mate, a coveted role to female wolves. But he had chosen her instead.

Cass had remained faithful to the pack, but the small lingering resentment simmered just below the surface. Nothing could be hidden from another member of the pack as the wolves' mind connection was that strong. Cass accepted her role after being rejected by the Alpha. Perhaps one day, things would change, but for now, she had become the pack Mother.

She turned away from the squirrel to return to the den. She didn't know that fate had a different plan for her.

***

Mr. and Mrs. Anderson drove deeper into the national park.

The thin two-lane road stretched ahead and behind for miles on end. In the back seat in a small crate, the two puppies climbed on top of each other, still trying to access their little mother, who was lying on the newspaper next to them. Small yips emitted from the cage, and Mrs. Anderson wiped away a tear as they continued down the road.

"Do you think we are far enough?" Mr. Anderson asked.

"I think so," she replied, suppressing her sadness. "There should be a pull-off soon, according to the map."

He reached over and placed a hand on her knee, a gesture that he wanted to be comforting. She pushed his hand away. Regardless of the circumstances and that their actions would save their reputation amongst their society friends, she didn't have to like it. She wanted to remain mad at him, at least for the day. She had told him already that it would help her get through what they had to do. They found the pull off, nothing more than a half moon of gravel against the forest's edge. She turned to face him.

"Can't we please reconsider?" she asked as one last plea.

"We've been over this," he said in a tone as gentle as he could muster. Truth was, he tired of his wife's sentimentality. The mongrels could drown as far as he was concerned. But his wife insisted they at least give them a fighting chance by releasing them at the side of the road. He opened his door and exited the vehicle. After pulling Bree from the cage, he clicked on the leash and handed it to his wife. She stood stoically by the side of the car with Bree at her feet, still wagging her tail and panting with the excitement of what seemed to be a day in the woods. Mr. Anderson took the puppies, one in each hand and all of them took off down the small path leading deeper into the forest.

Bree trotted happily between her humans. She could sense that the female seemed unhappy, but she couldn't venture to guess why. Her scent exuded sadness. Bree looked up at her with an open-mouthed grin. The man held the puppies, as well he should so they could have a nice view of the woods as they traveled along. Bree wouldn't have felt right had they been walking along with her. Soon they neared the creek. Bree happily lapped up the fresh, clear water running by as the humans stooped down at the edge. The floral scent of the forest soon became tinged with the female's tears, salty and sudden, causing Bree to lean on her knee and try to lick her face. *Don't be sad*, she wanted to say. *We are all here together, with the puppies even. Today is a good day.*

The man leaned down with her babies and set them at the foot of a large oak tree. The roots had reached through the earth and created a series of small caves and tunnels. He placed the two pups in one of these. The lady led Bree over to the small creatures, and she licked their heads each in turn. The puppies squirmed and yipped at her touch. Bree looked up at her humans. *Shall we walk more now?* she wondered. *Perhaps the puppies have rested enough and we can now go further.*

The man took a few steps down the path back toward the parked car. He turned to the lady who ran a finger over the forehead and nose of each of the pups. After what seemed like a long while, the lady also stood. With the leash in her hand, she walked toward the man and they both turned toward the car.

Bree trotted along for a few steps. Wait, she realized. They didn't get the puppies. Wait. She barked once, high and shrill to alert them of their mistake. The man would go back and get them once they realized. They both looked down at her and kept walking forward. Bree planted her feet. This wouldn't do. The lady pulled on the leash to guide her forward. Bree had always done as the humans had instructed. They were her pack and she was to follow them, but at this moment, they didn't seem to want to behave according to pack rules. She barked again, informing them that one of them must go back for the pups. She pulled against the length of the leash, but her feet took steps against the pressure.

"Bree, come!" the lady said. Against her will, Bree walked forward. The command voice took over and she responded on impulse. The car came into view. Bree struggled with her maternal instinct and loyalty to the humans. She pulled and whined, but the lady reached down and picked her up. The man unlocked the door and Bree was placed unceremoniously back into the crate, which still smelled of her puppies. As the small metal grate was clicked shut, she realized they would be leaving the forest without them. She strained to see out the window, but the only thing in her view was the heavy brown tree trunks drifting by as the car sped up down the road. The scent of her puppies began to fade as they drove farther, leaving her only with the old parchment scent of the newspaper in her crate.

***

The Mother knew she had ventured very close to the hard road.

In the far distance, she heard the noises of the flying dragon and caught the scent of humans as well. She would turn around and return to the den. Just as she did so, however, another scent invaded her senses. A scent that made her think about the lost fourth pup that had not survived long past his birth. She had managed to find a way to tuck that pain inside and surround it with the love of the other three, the love of the pack and the love of the Alpha.

If she could hide the pain, it would fade away and not weaken the pack in such a way as to jeopardize their safety. But what she sensed on the air made her stop and despite her better judgment, she considered going toward it. She smelled young canines. Newborn canines, by the tinge of milk on the air... but definitely not wolves. She sensed danger as well. Almost as soon as her mind registered this, the sound cut through the forest. High, shrill yips and cries soared through the branches around her. The maternal instinct overtook any sense of danger she may have felt toward herself. Immediately, she took off running toward the sounds.

What she came upon sent a shiver through the wolf's body. Her own pup had died of something natural, a problem with his nerves and muscles. Through her sadness over his death, she also knew that he wouldn't have survived long had he lived beyond that day. The forest teemed with predators, even for the wolves, who were feared by many of the creatures therein. What she saw before her was the sight of an eagle, which had landed on a domesticated puppy. Just to the left, barking and baring its small baby teeth in an effort to intimidate the bird, was another puppy, a sibling she knew from the matching scents.

Pure instinct drove her. Seeing the danger before her, she barked and jumped at the eagle. As it broke contact with the victim, the mother wolf placed herself between it and the injured dog. She bared her teeth, daring the predator to try for its lost prey. The eagle flew away, disappearing into the thick foliage.

The Mother turned to look over the injured puppy. She knew instantly that he couldn't be saved. The other dog, hopped closer, dodging forward and back again, wanting to see about his litter mate, but nervous about the wild beast guarding him. The mother wolf lay her head down on the puppy, licking his wounds. She gave a small submissive nod, just enough to let the other know that he could approach safely. He did so.

"How did you come to be here?" she asked, speaking to the small canine in her wolf way.

"The humans brought us here... then they went away with our mother."

They both stayed with the little puppy until he passed on. But soon, she felt the pull of the pack, as she had not returned within the time they thought she would. Her own puppies needed her, she knew. The Mother also sensed the Alpha connecting with her. He couldn't know exactly what she experienced, but he could sense that her reasons were important. She piled leaves on top of the prone body of the small dog and gestured to the other that he should return to the pack with her. He questioned this at first. The lady would return, he said. He should stay here in case they did.

No, their Mother explained the ways of humans. All she had known from them is their tendency to kill. Also, she admonished, the large ground dragons travel close to here. They decided to return to the pack. As she ran ahead, she realized that the small puppy had trouble meeting her pace. His legs were short like a cub. She returned and picked him up by his neck just as she would one of her own, and carefully stepped over the branches and brambles. They soon reached the clearing next to her den. The Alpha looked at her with consternation when she stepped forward with the puppy in her mouth. The mother placed the puppy carefully at the feet of the Alpha.

"What is this?" he questioned.

"We will call him Shadow, because I have a feeling that he will be my little shadow for a long time," she answered. She gave him a look that let him know that her acceptance of the puppy into her litter was not up for discussion.

Chapter Two

Soon enough, the wolf cubs explored the grove around the den for the first time in their little lives.

Alpha watched over them while Mother hunted for a meal. Shadow had lived with the wolf family for two moon cycles, and had been integrated into the litter as one of their own. After he had been found by Mother Wolf and taken into the den, he had welcomed the surrounding warmth from the other littermates. His hunger soon overcame him and he had nestled in with the others, finding sustenance and comfort. Mother Wolf could sense the Alpha's consternation at the new addition, but she knew that despite his initial misgivings, eventually, he would accept Shadow as one of their own.

In the short time, Shadow had grown accustomed to his brothers and sister. They had all opened their eyes and were allowed to venture out as far as the area around the den, but only under the watchful eye of one of the pack members. Sometimes it was Alpha or Mother, but sometimes, one of the others would keep them in sight. When they were old enough, Shadow knew that they would learn how to hunt in the forest, but for now, he enjoyed nothing more than to romp and play with his brothers and sister.

Blue, the cub with the blue-gray markings, Chase with the black markings around his eyes, and Snow, their sister with the white fur, all rolled and tumbled with Shadow. The ground beneath them yielded a soft bed of new green grass, edged in succulent flowers just at the edge of the tree line. After a good tumble and a playful snarl, his brother, Blue, stopped to look at Shadow thoughtfully.

"You're different from us, you know," Blue said. "Why is that, I wonder?"

"Am I?" Shadow said, looking down at his black curly fur. "How so?"

"You are smaller," Blue continued. His tone was not accusing, merely curious. "And your fur is different."

Shadow thought about this for a moment. "Yes, but Chase has different markings, and Snow's fur is also different. Yours is gray. Hers is white. Mine is just black. See? Not that different after all."

Blue considered. "Maybe, but you're shaped differently from us."

"Do you think so?" Shadow said, crouching down onto his paws. "But my teeth are the same as yours!"

He pounced onto his brother and the two rolled into a play fight as Shadow clamped down on Blue's scruff. They never bit hard enough to really hurt each other, and they both growled and laughed as they tumbled across the glen.

From nowhere, Snow plowed into the two of them, sending them into another frenzied roll. They didn't realize it, but the momentum sent them across the flowers and beyond the tree line. A sharp growl from Alpha alerted them, along with the mental jolt of the mind link.

"Until you're ready," Alpha scolded as they all slunk back into the grove, heads lowered and tails between their legs, "you must not leave this area. The branches overhead protect you from eagles, hawks and owls." Alpha's eyes burned into them, taking a moment longer when his gaze landed on Shadow. The memory had nearly faded, but Shadow felt that the connection had some kind of meaning to him, more than to the others. He didn't quite know why. Alpha continued, "The hunters never venture this far. As long as you stay in the grove, you will remain safe. Do you understand?"

They each nodded and waited for Alpha to dismiss them to play again. When he did so, Shadow felt the release of his mind from the fervent attention that he was forced to participate in when the Alpha demanded it. He connected with his littermates the most, but he was beginning to feel a slight connection with the other members of the pack. He already knew Thunder and Storm, two of the adult wolves that often hunted together. They sometimes watched over the cubs if Alpha and Mother had gone hunting. Cass, of course, and Elsa, the sister of Cass, also watched them. Shadow was only just beginning to feel the effects of being part of a pack.

"I wonder why we can't go past the edge of the grove," Chase said with a grumble after Alpha had sent them on their way. "What's so different about the forest?"

"We'll see when we are older," Snow said. "Storm says we will learn how to hunt and stuff."

"Like what stuff?" Shadow asked, bouncing ahead a few steps and then back again.

"You know," Blue said. "*Wolf* stuff."

"Like howling," Snow added, casting a sidelong glance at Shadow. "Do you think you would know how to howl?"

"Why wouldn't I?" Shadow said, drawing himself up to full height. "I could howl just like any other member of the pack."

Chase grinned. "Let's hear it, then."

Shadow thought about what to do next. He realized he did look different from the others. Their fur had a sleek finish and most of the pack had the markings of black, white or gray. His own fur had curls in it and was a deep shade of black. He wondered if the differences extended beyond that. What if he couldn't howl? he wondered. He had heard the others begin to practice lately, but he had been too afraid to try himself.

"You first, Chase," he said.

"Why should I go first? You've heard me howl."

Shadow changed his tactic. "But you are so good at it. I need you to show me how, just once. Come on Chase, please?"

"Okay, fine." Chase stepped forward into the middle of the group. Blue, Snow and Shadow looked on. Chase tossed his head in a

LITTLE WOLF

manner of clearing his throat. Then, he pulled his head back and let out a small squeak.

The others let out titters of laughter.

"I was just warming up!" Chase exclaimed with some embarrassment. He tried again, and this time, his voice came to him a bit stronger. His small, high-pitched howl rang across the glen, echoing off the trees on the other side.

Shadow watched in fascination. He would find a way to howl like that, he thought to himself. He would prove to them that he could be just as much of a wolf as any of them. The sound of the small howl seemed to inspire the others in much the same way as it had Shadow.

Snow stepped forward next to her brother and threw her head back. She emitted a low squeak and then another clearer cry, which harmonized with Chase's sound. Before another minute passed, Blue joined in. So far, he was the best of them all. Shadow finally succumbed and joined in. His own voice rang in a higher pitch than the others, punctuating the song with shorter utterances. He kept on, trying to mimic the haunting sound of his siblings. The sound of the four rang out across the glen.

They didn't know, but Mother had returned and had been watching them silently from the edge of the forest. A few moments later, she stepped forward next to Alpha. They both watched from the other side, beaming with pride as their little wolves practiced for the first time the sacred art: the howl.

Chapter Three

"Look alive, cubs!" Storm yelled as he ran with the litter through the forest.

The cubs had grown larger and were now allowed to run with the others. Each time they left the glen, they were assigned to one of the older members of the pack. Today, they ran with Storm, who goaded them into a fever pitch.

Shadow pulled hard to run as fast as the others. His siblings' legs had grown longer than his, but he discovered that he could still keep up and hold his own when they ran together. The other members of the pack tracked a small deer that had become separated from the others. If they succeeded in taking down the deer, this would be the littermates' first successful kill.

Shadow felt a surge of energy as he felt the adrenaline of the pack through the mind link, prompting his legs to run faster. Snow had dropped behind him and he felt her keeping pace at his heels. Blue and Chase paced alongside Storm.

Shadow caught the scent of the panicked prey as it stumbled through the forest. Its leg had caught on an exposed tree root and it fell. The pack members closest to her took the opportunity. Cass had the final kill this time, but the others circled in quickly. They waited first for the Alpha and Mother Wolf to have their portions. When finally given leave to do so, the rest of the pack finished the remaining meat. Shadow enjoyed the meal of fresh meat and the silent camaraderie of his pack mates around him.

After they had eaten, Mother quietly called the litter to her with a quick tug at their mental connection. Shadow and the others circled around her. The pack mates had begun to wander off, some taking the time to run alone. Others rested in patches of sun peeking through the branches.

"You may go on your own," she told them, "but you must return to the glen before the sun dips below the treetops. Don't go near the hard road, and stay away from the open spaces. If you see a human, return immediately to the grove. I will know and I will meet you there. Do you understand?"

"Yes, Mother," they said in chorus. Each of their tails wagged with anticipation of the new freedom that their mother was granting them. Shadow realized they had never run alone before, but he also knew she was testing them. If they didn't heed her warning, they wouldn't soon be granted such a privilege for a long while. Also, he had not been away from his siblings for any time that he could remember. With full stomachs and alert minds, they all scattered into the forest after Mother Wolf gave the final nod to dismiss them.

For a short while, Shadow walked along with Snow at his side. They walked in silence, sometimes exchanging a small thought with the other.

"Do you know where you will go?" Snow asked.

"No," Shadow said. "I guess I'll just see where the path takes me."

"I'm not going very far at all," Snow said. "Just because we can doesn't necessarily mean that we should."

Shadow wanted her to go on her own way. The need to explore on his own had pricked at his mind and when Mother Wolf had given them this permission, he wanted nothing more than the embrace of solitude.

"I'm going to see what I can find. See you later, Snow." Shadow could tell that they were farther from the den than they ever had been before. He knew that Snow wouldn't go much further. The little dog broke into a run, leaving his sister behind.

"Shadow!" she called out after him as he bounded over the tangled roots. "Shadow, wait! Don't go that way!"

Her voice quickly faded into the distance behind him as he gained speed. He didn't want to run as fast as he had during the hunt, but he kept a good pace. The trees jutted into the sky, making a canopy overhead.

The sunlight that did reach down to Shadow created patches of bright green, reflecting the light in ornate patterns on the forest floor. Shadow slowed to a walk to take in the view of the forest. A butterfly flitted by, which he followed, playfully bouncing toward it when it would alight on a leaf of underbrush. It amused Shadow to no end to watch the little insect fly away. He continued on, following a path that the forest dwellers had woven between the saplings. A human eye wouldn't have seen anything more than the brambles and roots of the forest floor, but Shadow stepped deftly along, following instinct and adventure.

After a while, he came upon something strange in the depths of the forest. An outcropping of rock jutted from the edge of an overgrowth of shrubbery. The scent surrounding the area was muted somewhat by the nearby stream, which added a musical melody to the sun-dappled forest. He looked over the rocks thoroughly, sniffing and peering at the strange arrange-ment.

Underneath the floral bright scent of the plant life and the fluid scent of the creek, another undercurrent met his senses, causing a feeling of confusion. The scent seemed very old, almost faded into nothingness, but Shadow recognized it as that of a human. Shadow could tell it had been a long while since any human had been there. The pile of rocks had such an intentional look about the formation that Shadow was not surprised to find this scent present. He felt alert already at being out for the first time on his own, but the reminder that humans had once been here heightened his senses even further.

Shadow circled around, finding that the area around the rocky outcropping consisted of smaller trees and heavy undergrowth. Tangled vines and brambles pulled at his fur as he carefully stepped through the small vale. He didn't know what he was searching out, and wondered if he should return to the den to tell Mother about his discovery.

No one thought that the humans would come this far into the forest, but it was clear, due to the degree of the scent level, that it would have been a very long time since a human had been there, perhaps even years.

He glanced at the sky. The sun still hovered well over the tree line. As such, Shadow decided that he would stay and explore a little while longer.

***

In another part of the world, one in which Shadow had existed at a time outside his memory, some people looked over a scrap of paper that represented the very patch of forest where he walked, discussing what was to happen with that belt of land.

"Right there," a man said, with a finger pointed to the very parcel on which Shadow explored. The old McDougall Farm, they called it, had just expired its historical protection. The land was now available for commercial property development. They could buy the land. The forest didn't exist under any park service. Just that little strip of it, between the overpass and the valley highway. The state would be expanding the road, bringing traffic through the area in the coming years. That land would be ideal for a commercial venture.

Of course, Shadow knew nothing of their plan. Nor did he know that the fate of his wolf family now hung in the balance.

***

Mother Wolf paced the grove, fretting and whining.

Alpha looked on with a small grin. "It is this way every season," he said. "You always worry, and they always return unharmed."

"Yes," Mother replied. "But that is not any guarantee that they will return *this* time." She glanced at the sky. "The sun is almost to the trees and they haven't yet returned."

"Almost to the trees," Alpha pointed out. "That is to say, not yet to the trees. They still have time." He walked over and nuzzled her shoulder, interrupting her nervous pacing. "Sit and rest," he said. "We have some time yet before they return. Let's enjoy the quiet while we can."

Mother stopped and turned her attention to her mate. "Perhaps you are right," she said. "The pack members have them well watched."

"Yes," Alpha replied. He turned and lay down in front of the den. With one last glance to the edge of the forest, she turned and joined him. Within moments, a little white patch of fur could be seen tumbling through the underbrush. Alpha smiled at Mother Wolf as, one by one, the pups returned to the glen. All except one.

"Where is Shadow?" Mother asked when Chase came back into the grove, still shaking off the drops of water from his apparent romp through the creek.

"I haven't seen him," Chase said. "I went on my own way."

"I saw him," Snow said. "Only for a little while, we walked together. He went that way." Snow nudged the air with her nose, indicating the direction.

None of the pups noticed, but Mother and Alpha gave each other a silent glance, exchanging a quick thought. It was put aside for a moment, however, because at that very moment, Shadow came through the thicket. He tumbled into the grove and shook off the leaves that had clung to his fur.

"There is the little adventurer," Alpha said as the last of the litter climbed into the den for the night's sleep. "Shadow, did you see anything on your explorations?"

"No, Father," he said innocently. "I just saw

regular forest stuff."

"Very well," Mother said, nudging him with her nose. "Sleep well, little cubs."

After the sun had sunk well below the trees and the sliver of a moon bobbed on the darkened treetops, and they were certain the pups were asleep, the Mother turned to Alpha. "We should tell them," she said.

"There is no need," the Alpha said with gentle sternness.

"It simply seems that we could avoid any chance of harm if we did," Mother insisted.

"It has been generations since any human has been in that part of the forest," Alpha continued. "The pups need not know of the past danger. It has passed. The family of humans has abandoned the farm long ago. I have checked carefully. There are no humans and no forgotten traps."

Mother set her chin on her paws. "Again, perhaps you are right. I worry about Shadow, though. The others can see that he is different from them. They notice his fur and his shape. He will not grow as big as the others. Not ever."

"That may be," Alpha said. "But don't worry. Shadow is just as much of a wolf as the rest of them. Or he will be."

"How do you know?" Mother asked.

Alpha laughed, low in his throat. "It was

you, was it not, who found him in the forest? Didn't you say that pup had faced off against an eagle nearly three times his own size? If he had that survival instinct as a young pup, then he is just as much wolf as any of us."

Mother leaned into him as they both began to drift off to sleep. "That is what worries me the most," she said. "That is exactly what worries me."

The two faded then toward sleep, keeping an ever-watchful sense on the safety of the pack, just under the surface of their restful state. As soon as Mother Wolf slept, the Alpha opened his eyes and turned his nose into the wind. The crescent moon shone down, a silver sliver in the indigo night sky.

Chapter Four

Months passed.

The wolves had grown, taking on the lanky shape of adolescence. Shadow had grown, too, though he still looked small next to the others, with his short legs and stubby nose. He had returned several times to the little area he had come to think of as his secret place. On various visits, he had found other things not native to the forest—a large wooden wheel nearly buried in the underbrush, several rusted metal tools, one that he had to be careful of as it jutted out of the ground at a dangerous angle.

Going there gave Shadow comfort in such a way that he couldn't quite explain, even if he had tried. The old and faded scent of the humans, only detectable with small concentration, tugged on his mind like finding an old forgotten plaything. He had not told any of his brothers or sister about the place, as he wanted to keep it to himself. He didn't know that on this day, he had been followed by one of his own pack. He trusted them all, even if he had known, but today, he would find that not all who seemed to be were his true friends.

Cass followed silently behind Shadow, keeping enough distance between them as to remain hidden and unheard. She suspected that Shadow's senses were not as sharp as her own since he was, in fact, not a wolf. Long ago, she had accepted the idea that Alpha had not chosen her as his mate. The Mother Wolf could have that duty, but Cass also knew that she could still be the mate of the pack leader if another wolf took on the role.

Alpha had been leader for a long time and she was not the only one who had begun to notice the white fur appearing at his muzzle. He had been a good leader and had protected them well, but every season must come and go. Cass knew it was time for youth to have its turn. Cass had taken to running with Storm during the hunt, and he had seemed receptive to her presence. They had formed the beginning of a friendship, though she could still sense his loyalty to the Alpha. If she could merely plant the seed of the idea, perhaps Storm would be convinced to, one day, challenge the Alpha. If he did so and won, then Alpha would have to submit to the new Alpha. And if that happened, he would return to being called by his previous name. Cass didn't know if anyone within the pack—except perhaps Mother herself—remembered the Alpha's prior name. No matter. He knew it. And one day soon, he would most certainly return to it.

Her yellow eyes glowed in the shadows as she crept along, shadowing the young male dog at a distance. Cass had noticed that Shadow sometimes liked to go off by himself. She had grown curious about the nature of these solo adventures. She watched as Shadow trotted along, carefully raising each paw higher than usual as he approached the thicker underbrush.

Cass watched the forest as they traveled, knowing by instinct and experience where they were. The trees stretched high overhead, but she knew that up above, they became shorter due to the time difference in overgrowth. She didn't remember a time when humans had walked this land, but she had heard the stories at the feet of the old ones before they had moved on.

As a young cub, she recalled the history being told to the pack, the thinly veiled warnings to avoid the place of the wall, as it had been called. This was a place of danger, she remembered. The story involved a dwelling with a presence of humans. Always dangerous, they said. The Old Ones had given them chills at night by recounting the story of Elder, who had ventured too close to the habitation and had received a wound by the human with a stick that made a loud cracking sound. Elder had made it as far as the edge of the grove before collapsing and dying, which was witnessed by the horrified eyes of the pack, as it had existed back then.

Since that time, the wolves had known never to set foot there again. But the humans had moved on, leaving the abandoned shell behind. With the last one gone, nature began to overtake the place. Roofs fell, walls collapsed. Time passed and the remains returned to the earth. All that remained now were some of the implements and the small rock wall, giving the area its name.

Surely, Cass thought to herself, Alpha and Mother Wolf had told their litter of this place. Warned them. Surely, Shadow knew not to go there. But as surely as they continued to move through the forest, his direction continued onward—right toward the place of danger.

Cass followed as closely as was comfortable and then stopped, letting her keen wolf vision watch as he moved toward the rock outcropping. She watched as he sniffed around, walking boldly toward the makeshift clearing. His happiness invaded the edges of her mind as he still had a presence with the mind lock, much to her chagrin. She knew that she remained hidden from him, as she had many years of practice ahead of him and her natural wolf abilities, as well. She wondered if she should alert Storm to come and join her, but she wanted to wait and see what else she could learn before sharing this with anyone.

Shadow strutted around, finding a stick and tossing it far enough to chase it down with a pounce. He repeated this play two or three times, before raising his nose to the air, as if he sensed her, but could not quite convince himself that she was there.

Cass crouched and made herself small in the shadows. She knew he wouldn't detect her presence by scent, as she had positioned herself downwind. *Silly little mutt*, she thought, *he will never survive in the pack, especially if he does not know enough to stay away from this place of danger.*

She scanned the area as she watched, her eyes landing on the strange blade that jutted out from the ground. She didn't know enough about humans and their practices to make any kind of guess as to what kind of tool it may have once been. But a plan began to form in her mind. Slowly, she stood, turning carefully so as not to disturb the leaves around her, and she returned to the usual territory of the pack.

Shadow played a bit in his secret place. He had come to love his time alone, away from the pack. He, of course, loved being with his family, but he sensed the differences between himself and the others. His moments of solitude allowed him to be himself in a way that he couldn't while in the presence of the others.

Shadow had known that someone followed him. He couldn't determine who, exactly, for they kept their presence hidden, even from his mind. But he moved forward as if unwatched. He had thought briefly about changing his route to the edge of the nearby creek, but he also knew that was where Chase liked to roam. Besides, he decided he didn't want to miss going to his secret place, simply to appease someone else. So, he went on.

The scent of the space seemed different today. Something had moved through the space since his last visit. He couldn't determine what, but the area was punctuated by a synthetic scent, quite unfamiliar to his senses. Shadow played, tossing around a stick for the amusement of anyone watching him. He sprang around, putting on the show of nothing more than a playful puppy.

Soon, though, he noticed that whoever had followed him had left. He pulled himself to full height, lifting his nose into the air to make certain he was alone. If so, he would go to the little place he'd found and have a nap. He didn't know that he was still being watched.

A man had come and carried with him a bundle of papers. On his head was a yellow plastic helmet that caused the synthetic scent that Shadow had noticed. The man wondered how the small dog had wandered out this far, noticing that he didn't wear a collar. The small canine looked like it had some kind of poodle in his breeding, though, clearly, it was a mutt. He watched as the dog wandered about, apparently as happy as could be, roaming around the area. After romping for a few minutes, the small dog curled up in what looked like the remnants of a small fireplace, not much more than a pile of rocks now. That was what had sent him here in the first place. He was to do some reconnaissance on the space, mainly to see what needed to be removed before they pulled the trees and plowed the land. They knew they had to remove some of the remaining evidence of the old farm before clearing the land.

For a while, the small strip of land had been

protected by a mostly unknown bylaw, allowing anything bearing historical remnants to remain untouched. The company that he worked for had been watching the clock for the time to run out. They had made a successful bid and it only needed to be accepted by the state for them to have full clearance to expand.

He had found evidence of rusted tools in addition to the old rock wall and fireplace. The foundation would have to be completely removed, erasing all evidence of the old farm. No matter, he thought. Everything had its season. He had no qualms about being part of the company that would take down part of the forest. It took up a huge swath of land and they would only be infringing on a small sliver of the parcel. He wondered what he should do about the little dog. He didn't know if he should try to get the dog to come to him, but decided against it, for now. Perhaps next time he came out, he would bring some treats, and try to befriend the little fellow.

The man turned and left the area. Next time, he would bring a wheelbarrow and some tools. They could go ahead and remove the metal and rocks, but they wouldn't be able to break ground until they received clearance that the bid had been accepted.

Shadow, oblivious to the man's presence,

dozed in the sun.

***

Cass bounded back to the familiar part of the forest, finding the scent of Storm and tracking him. She came on him sitting quietly on the edge of the meadow, staying in the shadows He greeted her with a perfunctory nuzzle when she walked up next to him.

"Where have you been?" he asked casually.

"I've been watching over Little Mutt," she answered. The wolves often watched over one or more of the younger ones.

"Don't call him that," Storm chastised. "He was chosen by the Mother and accepted by the Alpha. We must accept him as well. He is a pack member."

"It is true, but he is not a wolf."

"Perhaps not, but he is a pack mate and we should treat him with respect."

Cass stood silently as they both looked out over the meadow. "I understand that we must treat him like one of our own, but I am not entirely sure why."

"What do you mean?" Storm said.

"Well, someday, another wolf will take the place of the Alpha," Cass explained. "And each of us is being groomed to that event in one way or another, as is the way of a pack. Wouldn't you agree with that?"

"Perhaps," Storm said, watching her with a cautious eye. "What do you mean?"

"What place can a smallish dog hold in the pack, Storm?" she said.

"He can't be the Least Wolf. Mother Wolf would never stand for it. He is to be treated as one of her very own, not the lowest in the pack."

"I know that." She softened her tone and pressed her shoulder closer to Storm in a show of affinity. "Please don't misunderstand. I don't mean any disrespect toward little Shadow or anyone else. But I know I speak some truth. Shadow will never be equal to one of us. He will be tolerated, rather than respected."

Storm cast his eyes back to the meadow, eying a small woodchuck at the far edge of the clearing. "It will be many seasons yet before the Alpha will be replaced, if that's the intent of this conversation."

"Do you think so?" she said. "His muzzle is going white."

"You underestimate the Alpha."

"And you underestimate me." And then, she was silent.

The two continued to sit in silence, looking at the happenings of the meadow. Later, they would hunt. Cass felt satisfied with the first part of her plan. She knew that Storm shared her fondness. She trusted that in the right circumstances, she might be able to convince him that Shadow would never truly be one of the pack because he would never be able to measure up. This would take time and patience, Cass knew.

A flock of starlings flew from a low tree in the distance of the forest.

***

The next day, Steven Meadows returned to the job site to begin excavating some of the foreign objects that would hinder breaking ground on the location.

He had not thought much more about the little dog that he had seen the day before, outside of a passing thought that he might see the little fellow again. In the meantime, he would focus on the task at hand. He pulled the wheelbarrow out of the back of his pickup and started on the somewhat difficult task of pushing through the tangled forest to the job site. One day soon, he would have to bring a crew out to cut down a path. That would probably take a few days. A little less than ten yards in, he realized the error of his ways. He would have to leave the wheelbarrow for another day.

He returned to the truck and almost without thought, he grabbed the small bag of dog treats and headed back toward the site.

When he got there, there was no sight of the little dog, so he put the matter out of his mind and began to collect together some of the metal scraps. He had not heard yet if the bid would be accepted, but he figured there would be no harm in getting a start on clearing the area. The hike in was pretty lengthy on foot.

Once they had a path cleared, they would be able to drive in a cart until they had the land cleared enough for paving. In the meantime, he enjoyed the view. The sun still peered through the canopy of leaves above him, creating a dappled green glow as if light were shining through the stained glass of a cathedral. He could see that the trees had begun to thin, giving Steven the cue that he had arrived at the place where the old farm once stood.

He surveyed the area, the old rock wall, the pile of antique farm tools. He wondered briefly if the old tools would be worth anything. Surely, they must be worth something through some venue, but he didn't know enough about that sort of thing. He walked over to pick up a rusty piece of metal that looked like it had once been a blade to something. He tried to lift it but found it wedged into the ground enough that he would have to dig out around it.

A small noise caught his attention and he turned, thinking it may have been a squirrel or groundhog.

The little dog that he had seen the day before sat a little way off, just under a small tree.

"Oh, hey there, little fella," Steven said, crouching down.

The dog lowered his body, keeping a cautious pose, his eyes never wavering from the man.

Steven slowly reached into his pocket and withdrew a small treat, extending his hand out to the canine. The dog eyed him, keeping his eyes fixed on the human without looking once at the food in his hand. He had never seen a dog act that way before, and wondered again how the little guy had gotten so lost and ended up this deep in the woods. He tossed the treat and it landed nearly exactly between where he stood and where the dog crouched. Still, the dog didn't make a motion for it.

Steven took a step back, giving extra space to the dog, thinking that maybe he was shy. The dog just looked at him with the same unwavering gaze.

"Where'd you come from?" Steven asked.

Maybe the dog had been lost. If he could

find some way to identify him and turn him to the county animal control, then he could perhaps reunite him with his family. Surely, he belonged to someone. Steven took another step backward. His boot heel caught on a tangle of roots jutting out of the ground and he tumbled backward, landing hard on his backside. He sat up, rubbing his head and elbows.

"Ow!" he muttered. When he turned to look back at the tree, the little dog had vanished.

***

His tail between his legs, Shadow raced as fast as he could back toward the den.

He didn't know what to make of what had just happened. Of course, that had been a human. He could tell by the scent, but everything he had ever heard about them was that they were dangerous. This one didn't seem so. In fact, he had some kind of food.

Shadow also didn't know if he should tell anyone. If he did, they might decide to move the central den, which would mean travel and he would lose his beloved getaway. But if he didn't tell anyone and the human somehow posed a danger to the pack, Shadow could never forgive himself.

He ran on, bounding over the roots and

skirting under the low branches of the shrubbery. He ran for as long as he could before his legs began to burn with exhaustion. He slowed to a trot, glancing over his shoulder to make sure he had gotten clear. He saw no sign of the man, nor did he smell any scent of him in the light breeze. He must have left the forest.

"What did you find, little one?" Cass's voice startled Shadow and he turned on his heels, coming to a full stop to face her. She had stepped out of the trees close to him and had approached unseen.

"What do you mean?" he said, his mind racing to think.

"You seem agitated," Cass said, referring to her ability to sense his emotions through pack empathy. "I simply ask why."

"I'm not agitated," Shadow said, pointing his head up and away from her. "I was just running."

"Running from what?" Cass asked again. "What are you afraid of, little one?"

Shadow turned toward her, irritated. "I'm not afraid of anything!" he insisted. Shadow had sensed Cass's cool demeanor for a while and sometimes wondered what he might have done to invoke her ire. Cass, however, smiled at his outburst.

"It's all right, Shadow," she said. "I meant

no disrespect. Let us go back to the grove together. The others are gathering for a hunt soon, and I am certain that you are hungry."

Shadow walked in silence alongside the female wolf. Cass, being his elder, demanded that he treat her with a certain element of respect, but Shadow's place as part of the Alpha's offspring also allowed him certain privilege within the placement of the pack, which Cass had no choice but to respect. They walked along in the quiet of the forest.

Shadow looked forward to the hunt, for Cass had been right. He did feel quite hungry. The thought made him wonder if she had seen what had happened with the human. He had offered Shadow food, that much was certain. Shadow wondered if any of the others had experienced anything like that from a human before. He glanced at Cass, who trotted just ahead. She had caught the scent of some of the other pack mates, as had Shadow. She tossed back her head, emitting a short howl to alert them of her presence.

The return response sounded like a chorus of music, each voice unique in its own way. Thunder's voice range was low and pure, while Storm had a higher sound, a knife-like pitch cutting through the stillness of the forest. Of course, Alpha and Mother both joined in the refrain with their confident vocalizations, drawing everyone near to the grove.

They gathered without a spoken word between any of them. The younger ones had heard the howls and soon bounded into the grove to join the others. When preparing for the hunt, each of them allowed their minds to open to benefit from the shared alertness and keen senses of the others. During this time, more than any other, Shadow truly felt as if he were part of something greater than himself. They were all present, the pack fully accounted for.

Alpha stood strong and silent, looking over his charges. Shadow saw Snow dancing on her front paws in anticipation as the energy built. Mother had raised her nose into the air, waiting to catch the scent of something. As if on an unseen cue, they all bolted at the same time, leaping as one into the dense woods. Shadow felt himself cut through the foliage, surrounded by the sleekness and blood desire, along with the others. Snow ran to his left and Chase to his right. Just behind him, he sensed Blue keeping pace.

As of yet, the older members of the pack stayed to the outside of the formation as a means of protecting the young ones in the middle. During some of the more recent hunting excursions, Shadow had noticed that this protective formation had become looser. Perhaps, he thought, he and his littermates were becoming skilled enough that they needed less protection.

He ran, awaiting the sound of the howl that communicated to the others that they had caught the scent. Shadow stretched out his mind to see what the others could see. Nothing, yet. Squirrels, birds, yes, but so far, no deer or elk to fill the stomachs of the entire hungry brood. His mind quickened as he sensed Thunder had scented an elk in the distance. The scent of the creature pierced through the pack inciting them with new excitement and fervor.

The mood intensified. The others pulled in as if they became a single arrow aiming for the heart of the creature they planned on felling for their cause. The doomed elk couldn't yet be seen and probably had no knowledge of the pack. Yet. As they closed in together, Shadow could see an image in his mind, the plan of attack springing from the mind of Alpha to all of them within close proximity. This way, they would know the others' movements, even as they separated to circle the prey.

Shadow saw the path he would take, a small part in the larger plan, each of them with their own role. He would circle around to the front, as the necessary distraction before the larger wolves homed in and brought the elk down. Mother would take the kill this time, the plan was decided, and they would all have their fill.

The pack separated, each wolf falling into the places determined by the plan in place. Everything faded away. Shadow felt as if the trees themselves vanished as he moved forward. He focused his mind on the presence of the elk, standing still at the edge of the lake, head lowered to the water to quench his thirst.

Shadow broke to the left in a smooth motion, muscles working, sinew stretching and contracting as he ran. With deft footing, he neared the unwary creature. The elk raised his head, suddenly aware of something amiss. But he didn't sense Shadow, though, nor the other wolves. Shadow circled the thicket closest to the lake, bringing the elk into view. The massive creature towered over the edge of the water, his antlers reaching for the cloudless sky that was reflected in the water. It had turned but not toward Shadow.

The large creature's gaze cut back across the forest beyond where the wolves approached. He didn't know what had alerted the elk, but within seconds, it broke into a run, away from the water's edge, and away from the approaching pack.

Shadow pulled his speed to a quicker pace.

He could still make it around to the front of the animal and slow his escape, allowing the others to complete the circle and take him down. But it was not meant to be. Shadow pulled alongside the panicked elk, whose feet dashed forward. In a last effort, Shadow tried to lunge for the nimble ankles, but at the last moment, the elk bounded over him and escaped up the mountainside, disappearing into the pines.

The prey was lost. Lost!

"Good going," said Chase, his voice drenched in sarcasm, as he walked up and paced alongside of Shadow. They all knew at once the moment the elk had escaped and a surge of disappointment washed through the pack.

"What are we going to eat now?" Snow chimed in.

Blue had little to say, but he cast a sympathetic eye toward Shadow.

Shadow gave them all a sidelong look. He felt angry. Something had alerted the elk to their presence, but it was not him. He knew he had had a clean path to his desired location around the other side, but he had been so focused and in tune with the pack mind that he had not heard the same noise as the elk. *What was it,* he wondered.

His answer came from Alpha, who stepped up to Shadow, facing the same way that the elk had escaped. Shadow could sense the disappointment and frustrations coming from the other pack members, but Alpha soon put them to rest.

"The loss was no fault of Shadow's," he said with finality. "What the creature heard came from an intruder into our forest. Humans. The humans have entered our land, beyond that which the hunters roam. The forest has been compromised."

The wolves all looked toward the Alpha with horror. This time, it was different, they knew, though they didn't know how. The Alpha gazed out over them with a look of knowledge. "The old ones told the stories of the time of the humans. Once, we roamed the forest as far as the eye could behold. There were not hard roads, or growling machines that tormented our numbers. Once, the wolves were the royalty of all the animals of the forest. We could hunt as we pleased. The humans traveled in packs, much like our own, and we lived in honor and respect for each other."

The others settled in around the Alpha as he continued the story.

"So, long ago, the humans and the wolves almost lived side by side, one never bothering the other, but sharing the land with each other and the many animals. Our numbers were many. We are one pack, but during this time, a single pack could number as much as ten times as large as ours."

"What happened to us all?" Blue asked with a tentative voice.

"More humans came," Alpha said. "Different than before. Their coats and fur looked different than what we had seen before. They had strange branches that exploded and caused us to fall to the ground. Over time, they changed the land. First, they came with horses, not the wild ones, but others who served them. And with those horses, and they cut down the trees by the hundreds and dragged them away until the forests were thin.

"They killed off many of the other animals, down to such small numbers that they almost vanished completely. Then they began to change the paths, turning them into the hard roads that you have seen. The buildings and the outside world became more and more plentiful, pressing our places of living smaller and smaller.

"What we have now, this vast forest, is merely a parcel of land, compared to how it once was. I fear…" Alpha began this last statement looking away from them, avoiding all of their eyes. "I fear that the humans that come this time would do so again. These are not the hunters who can be frightened away with a mere glance. These are the humans that will come with the destroyers and take down the trees and dig up the ground. We cannot frighten them. We cannot run from them. We cannot escape what will happen if these humans come into the forest."

He stopped speaking and looked at them each one in turn. His deep golden eyes glinted in the setting sun, reflecting the orange glow. Shadow had never seen such sadness as that which was reflected in his father's eyes in that moment. Little did he know that the sadness they all felt at that point in time would pale and vanish before the day's end.

Chapter Five

The wolves returned together to the relative safety of the grove.

"What shall we do, then, before the humans come?" Thunder asked in a wild bid for attention among the squabbling voices of the pack.

"We must travel deeper into the woods," Cass said, a slight edge of panic in her voice.

"We cannot," Mother responded. "The trees grow thick there and food is scarce."

"It is scarce enough here!" Cass said. The voices jumbled together as the adult wolves all vied for the center of attention.

"That's enough!" Alpha finally bellowed.

The pack fell silent at this command.

He lowered his voice when he continued,

"That is enough. Yes, it is true that we lost a good kill today. It is also true that the presence of the humans alerted the elk and that is what sent him running before we had a chance to circle in. But we must not panic. I have known about the human's presence for a little while now."

Shadow and Snow exchanged a shocked glance. He had *known?*

Alpha gave them all a stern look as he continued, "I haven't yet made a decision as to how the pack will deal with this new circumstance..."

"We should move up the mountain..." Cass said.

"Take a stand, is what I say," Thunder added. "Fight them!"

"No," Mother Wolf said. "It's too dangerous."

"We need to wait and see how this plays out," said Storm. All of the voices blended together in a cacophony of heightened emotions.

"However," Alpha said in an authoritative tone, which silenced them once more. "However, I will take into consideration everyone's position. For now, the pack must eat. We can each hunt on our own as the smaller creatures are not as alert and will be easier to track. We all know where the plants and berries are as well. Yes, I realize it is not fresh elk, but it will have to do." Alpha nodded, indicating that he had dismissed them. He turned his back as, one by one, the pack members left the grove to find their own small meals.

Shadow silently watched. He had never seen the looks on the faces of the other adults and wondered if this pack had ever faced such a situation before. The sound of his stomach growling brought his attention back to the issue at hand. Like the others, he needed to eat. He watched them go, one by one. Finally, only he remained, aside from Mother and Alpha. Then, even Mother finally left the grove, after a quick touch of the nose with Alpha.

Shadow waited quietly watching before he took a step to leave and find food.

"Shadow." Alpha spoke without turning toward him.

"Yes, Father," he said, expecting some chastisement for losing the elk.

"You would have had him, you know, if he had not gotten spooked."

"Yes, I know," Shadow replied. "Thank you, Father."

Shadow exited the grove and let the thicket of the underbrush embrace him as he wandered, not entirely sure where he would go. He sensed the others walking away on their own, each of them grateful for the solitude after the day's disappointments. Shadow had run a lot that day already. He didn't want to exert much more energy to go after a squirrel or other small creature. It would be better than nothing, he knew, but the fight had gone out of him.

He wandered without thought, nibbling on some berries alongside the forest floor. Suddenly, a thought entered his mind. He knew where he could find some food. The small parcel of meat that the man had offered. The human had tossed it to the ground. It would only be a mouthful, but perhaps it would give him enough energy to be able to seek out another animal after he ate it. Besides, Shadow knew that the man had more food. He had only just given him one of them, but Shadow had noticed by the scent that the man had a small bag of them in his pocket.

I should avoid the area, Shadow thought. *Humans are dangerous*. In the end, hunger won out and Shadow headed toward the place of the wall to find the morsel of food.

When he arrived there, he sensed no sign of the human, except for the imprint of the scent left from his contact with him earlier. Shadow glanced around the area, pinpointed the small bite of meat and stepped forward to grab it. He had no more than pulled the bit with his tongue and begun to chew, when a firm hand landed on his neck, grabbing him by the scruff.

Shadow quickly scrambled backward, trying to escape the intrusion, but the human had him firmly by the neck. A large box with a metal grate door sat nearby and Shadow quickly figured out what was to happen to him. He wriggled his legs, kicking and twisting with all the strength he had, but the darkness of the enclosure encircled him.

Shadow let out a long warning howl to alert the others. In one sound, he sent the message: *Danger!* The others heard. Snow had been closest and as soon as she heard the high-pitched sound, her hackles raised. She sounded the alarm to amplify the warning to any who might be further off and not have heard the original call of warning from Shadow.

Further along, Blue picked up the sound and amplified it with his own howls. Soon, the chorus was filled with the voices of Cass, Storm, and Thunder. Mother ran back to the grove, bounding through the trees just as Alpha stepped out of the den.

"Shadow," she said, voicing what they all already knew. "They have Shadow. The humans have Shadow!"

Alpha tried to calm her, placing his chin

over the back of her neck in the wolves' embrace. "These are difficult times," Alpha said. "We must all be careful now."

Mother buried her face into the silver coat of the Alpha, knowing, in that moment, that there was nothing that could be done. The continued sound of the pack's mournful howls echoed through the expanse of the forest. All of the creatures stopped to listen. Every bird fell silent. Creatures in the underbrush stood still, peering up over the short growth. Even the larger creatures that usually feared the wolves heeded the cry. They all heard and they all understood. The human had entered the forest and had taken one of them. And they knew that nothing would be the same for any of them, not ever again.

Alpha kept his comforting presence by his mate as she cried into his shoulder, but his thoughts were veering toward how to best take care of the pack. He had suspected from the beginning that Shadow would one day be a liability to them. When his mate had brought Shadow to the den, it had been immediately clear to him that Mother wouldn't accept anything less than his full acceptance of the adoption of the lone pup. Perhaps he should have refused the pup from the beginning.

No use in dwelling on it now, he thought to

himself. The past has already transpired. Now, he had the task of considering what would be the best course of action to keep the rest of the pack safe. They would mourn, of course, as they would for any fallen pack member. Then after the allotted time, they would most likely travel, relocating the den to a more remote location, further up the mountainside.

One where the humans could never, ever follow.

Chapter Six

Shadow crouched in the small cage, the motion of the vehicle throwing him from side to side as they traveled along the road.

He recognized the scent of the man who had grabbed him as the same one from before. After placing him in the crate, he had tossed in a few more bites of the strange treat from before, but Shadow ignored these—they laid untouched in front of him on the cold plastic floor of his small enclosure.

As far as he could tell, the man was the only one present in the vehicle with him. The motion of the travel brought up another distant memory that Shadow couldn't quite identify. He wondered with a deep pang if he would ever get back to the pack, and if any of them were in danger from this thief. For indeed, Shadow had been stolen. He had heard the echo of Snow's howl, so he knew the warning had gotten out to the others. The motion stopped. They had arrived somewhere. The crate moved again, and he felt a jolt as the crate was placed on a surface of some kind.

He heard the human voices speaking outside the crate, but Shadow didn't understand their staccato words. They sounded like the birds of the forest, making sounds that just piled on each other with no sense of poetry or purpose. He could make out the tone if he concentrated enough. The man, the one who had captured him was telling the other, perhaps a female, about how he had lured Shadow with food and then stolen him from his family.

The female human seemed receptive to the information. Her scent indicated that she might be an ally of some kind, if such a thing was possible with the humans. Shadow had no doubt that he would find a way to escape and get back to the pack before the day was out. The humans had finished talking, it seemed, and the crate had been lifted once more. The door opened and a face appeared and looked inside at him. Shadow suppressed the feeling of panic that he felt at the scent of her because something else had caught his attention.

Behind the female, he could make out what seemed like bare walls, a small bench, nothing more than a wooden board nailed against the wall, and two small bowls. One had been filled with water, and the other, Shadow saw, was full of something that smelled like it was supposed to be food. Not the fresh meat of a recent kill, of course, but something edible anyway. His mouth watered at the scent, but he held back. He decided to take a chance and dart out of the open gate to get past the female human.

He managed to do so, but found himself no more escaped as he was in the closed room with no open door. He darted around the room, looking for an opening of any kind, but found no means of escape. Shadow turned toward the female and bared his teeth, his hackles raised. If he couldn't escape, then he would let her know that he was not happy to be there.

He tried to make himself as large as he could, and he felt pleased when she lowered herself down, becoming smaller. She put her hands behind her back for a moment and he didn't see until too late, the small object in her hand as she reached for him. The pinching sting in the side of his rump was quick and when she pulled back, he tried to snap at her, his teeth clicking together against thin air. The room suddenly felt thick and moved in much the same way as when he had been inside the vehicle. His legs swayed, then eventually gave way as his vision went black.

***

"Well, would you look at that," he heard a voice say as if from a great distance. "He's trying to wake up. Boy, he's got a lot of fight in him."

Shadow didn't know how much time had passed when he opened his eyes. He had been locked in a small cage with open metal bars on either side. The voice he had heard came from a female dog who inhabited the cage next to him. Beyond that, he could see more cages, each containing one dog. The female who had spoken had long, light-brown fur and ears that dusted the ground on either side of her front feet. She had a friendly face, but Shadow remained wary.

"You feeling okay there, Tiger?" she asked.

"My name is Shadow," he mumbled. "What is a tiger?"

She chuckled. "Where are you from?"

He didn't reply as he painfully pulled himself up to look around. The bowls of food and water had been placed against the back wall, and the presence of it reminded Shadow of how long it had been since he had eaten.

The other dog let out a small laugh. When she spoke again, Shadow noticed that her language had a strange lilt to it that was much different than the wild wolves of the forest. "It's nice to meet you, Shadow. I'm Lila. And you can eat what's in the bowl. It won't hurt you."

"She's right. It's not bad, once you get used to it," said another dog on the other side. Shadow turned to see a large white short-haired canine peering at him through the bars on the other side. He jutted his nose toward Shadow's full bowl. "Name's Gilroy. Pleasure to make your acquaintance."

Shadow said nothing.

"I'm not so sure, Gil," Lila said. "This one's feral. I can tell by his voice and by the way he carries himself. He's been in the wild for a bit. How long have you been in the wild, Mutt?"

"It's Shadow," he said.

"Wild, eh?" Gilroy said, his voice low and suspenseful. Something about him made Shadow think he didn't quite believe him. "How long, eh? Did you have a family before? Did they give you the shoulder tag? If you have a shoulder tag, they can find your family again. No matter how long it has been."

"What's a shoulder tag?" Shadow asked.

Both dogs laughed, and Lila spoke. "Wow, you have been out for a while. How long has it been since you've had a family? You look pretty well fed. You need a bath and a brushing of course, but you look as if you've eaten as recently as yesterday. If you're lost, then who's been feeding you?"

Shadow considered the words she spoke. "I don't understand. I hunt."

They didn't make sense to her, but the other dog nodded along and listened intently when she stopped her questioning, waiting to hear the answer. Shadow was not sure how much he wanted to share with his new acquaintances, so he walked over to his bowls. The water smelled mostly like water, a little stale compared to the fresh creeks and lakes he was used to. But he sensed no danger and drank.

"Where are our manners?" Lila exclaimed. "Gilroy, he's probably starving. We should let him be until he gets oriented. Listen, honey," she said, turning back to Shadow. "If you have any questions, any questions at all, you just ask Aunt Lila, okay?"

Shadow glanced at her, nodded to alleviate her maternal gaze and perhaps offer himself a bit of silence. His head hurt a little and he hoped that maybe a bit of water and some food would help. This place looked and felt completely strange to him. He didn't know what to do. As far as he could tell, the cage couldn't be breached. He sniffed at the strange substance in the bowl before him. It smelled somewhat like something that may have been meat at one point in time. But finally, hunger overcame him and he ventured a small bite. It seemed palatable, but, by no means, any comparison to anything he had eaten in the past. Once his stomach felt satisfied, he looked through the bars to see what the surrounding room looked like.

Next to him on either side were the dogs that he had already met. Lila had curled up on the small pillow in the corner of her own cage. Gilroy stood with his nose pressed against the bars along the path between the cages, his tongue lolled out and eyes darting back and forth, as if waiting for something. Shadow couldn't guess what he could possibly be waiting for.

Beyond each of them, he could see more dogs, all different shapes and sizes. Each of them seemed occupied with their own activity, as if they existed on their own. Some of them barked seemingly at nothing, while others slept and others played. Some had small toys that they tossed about in the small space. Shadow remained baffled as he looked around. What was this place? How could the other dogs exist with such a seeming acceptance of the sounds and horrible smells of their spaces? In fact, this place was the worst thing he had ever smelled, and that included the breath of buzzards.

Shadow paced back and forth. Whatever had been in that sting to his hip had obviously made him fall asleep for a while. He had noticed when he had awakened that he had a strange strap fastened tightly around his neck. A small metal circle hung down onto his chest. He found it rather annoying but he had noticed that all of the others had a similar contraption wrapped around their necks. He shook his head, wondering if that action would loosen it in any way, but it remained firmly attached. The barking at the far end of the room increased as some commotion happened. The door at the far end of the pathway had opened, and Shadow could tell right away that humans had entered the space. He pulled himself back into the far back edge of the cage, in an attempt to hide.

Lila gushed, "Look lively. Now's our chance."

"Our chance for what?" Shadow asked, cutting his eyes in her direction. She stood at attention with her tail wagging. Shadow thought the wagging was to such an excess that he was not sure if she could remain standing.

"To find a family!" she said. "If you've got a tail, wag it."

"I have a family. My pack."

"I'm talking about a human family, son. It's time to turn on the charm!" She hopped about the cage, shaking her ears and never ceasing the tail-wagging.

He looked over to exchange a sympathetic glance with Gilroy, only to find him in much the same state. The humans continued down the hallway, stopping at each cage and peering through to whatever canine stayed within. All of them, Shadow noticed were running in circles, jumping, placing paws on the bars of the cages, but the element that baffled Shadow the most was that each of them seemed desperate for the attentions of the humans. He placed his own chin down on his paws. *What sort of place had he found himself in?*

"My family is in the forest," he mumbled to no one in particular. He felt certain that no one would hear him in the havoc. He watched as the mayhem continued, finally drifting off to sleep, despite the noise.

Chapter Seven

Shadow could tell by the darkness of the room that night had come.

Many of the dogs in this strange place had fallen asleep. Shadow stood up and stretched. After examining his cage and determining that it remained remarkably unchanged, he decided to try something. Ever since he had been taken from the forest, he had lost the mind link to the pack. He felt it fade away, the further the vehicle had gone, and now that he had a moment of near-silence in which to contemplate his situation, he felt the profound loss of the connection.

After a quick visit to the water bowl, he sat down on the cold floor next to the pillow. He didn't like to sit on it, as it smelled like other dogs, most likely those who had come before him. He closed his eyes and concentrated. He pictured in his mind a light emanating from his forehead, reaching out to the others.

He tried his best to see Mother resting in the den, her watchful eyes roaming the space outside the opening. He saw in his mind's eye, Alpha pacing the grove, pressing the grass into a flat carpet with his large padded feet. Shadow tried to touch their minds with his own, but the distance was just too great. He opened his eyes and placed his chin on his paws, wondering if he would ever see his family again.

Hello.

Shadow lifted his head and looked around. Seeing and hearing nothing, he lay his head back down.

Hello, are you there?

He didn't know where the sound was coming from. Not really even a sound, just a presence in his mind somehow.

Hello. The nudge came again.

Shadow had no idea where it could be coming from. Tentatively, he tried to offer a mental response. *Who are you?*

Who are you? the little voice replied. *You reached out to me, remember?*

I was trying to reach my family, Shadow replied. *Wait a second, are you here? Where are you?*

Where does your family live?

In the forest, he replied. *What is your name?*

What's a forest?

What do you mean, 'What's a forest?' Don't you know?

No, I don't have a family yet. I came here with my littermates. I don't know very much.

Littermates? What's your name, little one? Shadow asked again.

There was a long silence. Shadow had begun to think that the connection had somehow been broken. The rustling of dogs moving here and there, an occasional whine, the sound of a metal bowl scooting across the cement floor. All sounds could be heard except the small voice. He peered around, trying to see through the bars to the other dogs within the compound. Was she there somewhere, he wondered. Was she within the walls of this room? He had nearly given up. He couldn't reach his family, perhaps he could no longer reach this connection either.

Ula.

Finally, his answer came.

My name is Ula.

Chapter Eight

Shadow awoke the next morning when another human female came in and turned on the lights. As soon as the lights came on, a large commotion of barking and chaos began once more. The human walked to the far end of the row and opened a cage, taking the dog out of the cage with a lead and walking back down the hall. A few minutes later, the human and dog returned. She repeated the process with the next dog in the row, opening the cage, taking out the dog and leaving, only to return a few minutes later. One by one, she came down the row, closer and closer to Shadow's cage. He wondered what he would do once she reached him. Maybe this could be an opportunity to try to get out. To where he didn't know, but he knew he had to try.

Good morning.

The intrusion into his mind startled him and reminded him of the mental connection he had made the night before. Not knowing the origin of the little voice disoriented him and made him feel frustrated, which she must have sensed. He felt a trill of laughter and another reply.

I'm three cages behind you to the left.

Shadow turned and stretched his vision as far as he could through the disorienting bars, which seemed to weave together, making it difficult to get a clear view. He wondered briefly why he had not made a connection with Lila or Gilroy. They both still lay sleeping in their respective cages, despite the growing din of the waking dogs.

Shadow paced the small space. Finally, he caught a glimpse of a small black and white dog standing at the edge of her cage. She looked at him, tail wagging, tongue out with a relaxed expression on her face.

Ula, is that you? he said, reaching out with his mind.

It is me. She spun in a circle, the pace of her wagging increasing, once she caught sight of him.

What's happening? he asked. *Where is the*

human taking the dogs?

Just the morning walk. That's all. The human takes all the dogs out, one at a time, to go up and down the path. Then back again. It's kind of nice to be out of this room.

Is there a way out?

Why would you want to get out?

I have to get back to my family.

Oh, you have a family. I see.

Her thoughts took on a tone of sadness at the suggestion of a family. Their conversation was cut short, however, because at that moment the human female opened the cage door and locked the end of the leash onto Shadow's collar. Before he made it out the door, he received one last warning from Ula.

Just go along with everything for now. Don't fight the human. No one is going to hurt you....

The next thing Shadow knew, he was quickly led through the open door and into a hallway. The walls and floor didn't look much different than those inside, but he saw sunlight streaming through the small windows on a double door at the far end of the corridor. It was toward this double door that they walked.

Shadow took a moment to consider the scent of this human. She was one that he had not seen before, and she exuded confidence and a sense of comfort toward the animals. He could tell that she didn't intend to hurt any of them. He became curious, as his thoughts tumbled together in an attempt to make sense of all of it, why someone who seemed to care about the dogs would stand by while they lived in cages, kept away from each other or from going outside.

When they arrived at the door, the human female pushed open one side with her hip and led him out with a careful tug on the leash. He considered Ula's last bit of advice and walked forward, letting the human guide him.

They stepped into a courtyard that was covered in grass and surrounded by a tall chain-link fence. He wouldn't be able to get over that. He had once seen Thunder clear a stand of wood and wondered if his old pack mate would find a way over this fence, but a pang of sadness made him push the thought out of his head.

Briefly, he wondered what his pack—especially Snow, Chase, and Blue—might be up to at this moment. The human reached down and with another click, unhooked the leash. Shadow stood for a moment, unsure what to do next. The female snapped a sharp but friendly command at him, one that he didn't recognize. He turned his gaze up to her to see if he could figure out what she wanted, and when he did so, she threw something quickly across the space.

Shadow followed the item with his eyes, a small round object that bounced and rolled ahead of them. He only found it mildly interesting. It wasn't prey, so why bother?

A large blue jay flew into view and perched atop the fencing around the courtyard to watch and mock him. As jays did.

"She wants you to run after it," the jay chirped in a mocking, almost sarcastic tone.

"Run after it?" Shadow replied.

"Yeah," he said, tossing his crested head. "Chase it and take it back to her. If you humor her, they are more likely to treat you fairly. You have the look of 'wildness' all over you. Those of us who know it can see it on you, but the humans might just think of you as a problem dog. You need to learn to play the part of a friendly dog."

Play the part, the bird had said. *Go along with everything,* Ula had told him. This whole place seemed strange to him, but he thought perhaps these other animals had been there far longer and may have gained some wisdom for survival.

"Why are you helping me?" he asked the bird.

The blue jay cocked his head to the side and let out a loud screech that may have sounded like laughter. "For my own amusement." With that, he raised his wings and fluttered off. *Free.*

Shadow considered his choices. The human had been making soothing, clucking sounds and waving her arms toward the ball where it had rolled to a stop, not far from the edge of the courtyard.

Shadow took a breath. He took off in a light sprint. He grasped the ball in his teeth and returned it to the human, dropping it at her feet in much the same way he had remembered the older pack members dropping food in front of Mother when she had still been nursing the pups. To his great surprise, the human female exclaimed with a joyful voice and placed her hands behind his ears, scratching and rubbing at his fur. He had never felt anything like that before. It felt… glorious.

For the first time since he had been taken from the forest, he felt a moment of happiness.

Was that all it took? A scratch of the ears? He felt ashamed, as if he were betraying himself by enjoying her touch.

She picked up the ball and threw it again. This time, Shadow followed its trajectory and caught it at almost the same time that it landed. He returned it to the human and was pleased when she scratched his ears once more. They played the game for a little while. He did something for her and then, she did something for him. He fetched. She praised and scratched his ears. Then she took him back on the leash and led him around the other side of the building.

Right away, Shadow could tell by the overlapping scents of this new patch of grass that the human intended for him to relieve himself here. His mind reeled with confusion. Many dogs had done so, despite the clear message that whoever had been here first had claimed the plot as their own. Shadow hesitated, but it had been a while and he did need to answer the call of nature. He glanced at the leash around his neck. The human seemed to be waiting for him to do something.

He gingerly took a step forward, careful to avoid any movements that might soil his feet with the dirt of another dog. Finally, he found a small corner in which he could do what he needed to do. He desperately wished that the human would give him some privacy, as he didn't care for an audience even outside of his species. Her presence added to his humiliation, but he avoided her eyes as he crouched to relieve himself.

Back inside the building, he was placed back in his cage. He noticed that the food and water had been refilled. He glanced around.

Lila had awakened on her pillow. Gilroy had gone with the human woman, as he was next in line. Shadow made a brief reconnect with Ula across the way and waited to see what would happen next.

Hours seemed to pass by. Besides the idle chit-chat with the others, Shadow thought that the boredom would overcome him. He had slept as much as he could, but there seemed to be no other way to pass the time. Once he had returned from outside, the noisy din of the room had ruined any attempt to reconnect with Ula, and he wondered what sort of life she had prior to coming to this place. Perhaps he would ask her tonight if they connected again after the quiet of night fell on the room. Little did he know that the chance would never come.

After all of the dogs had been taken out and brought back again, Shadow noticed that other humans started to come into the room. Some came alone, others came in small groups, many with small human-cubs with them. Each time one of these groups came into the room, the other dogs would fall into such a noisy frenzy that Shadow wondered a bit at their sanity. No Alpha quieted them. Not even a human one.

The human man arrived about mid-afternoon. Shadow recognized him immediately when the female human let him through the door. They walked to his cage and exchanged some words. He watched, cautious but curious at what might happen. This was the same man that he had seen in the forest, in what felt like ages ago. It had only been days, Shadow realized.

Once more, the female human reached inside and clipped the leash on his collar. Shadow's instinct made him want to pull against the offending binding, but he recalled the advice of his friends again and followed along when led out of the cage. They returned down the path to the door into the hallway. Only this time, instead of turning toward the double door to the courtyards, they went the other way into a bright sunlit room that seemed to have fresh air in it.

The female handed the leash to the man and gave him a shoulder bag that sagged under the weight of the contents. He hitched the bag onto his shoulder and said a few friendly-sounding words to Shadow.

Shadow followed the man out the door and back into the same vehicle that had taken him from the forest.

The idea crossed his mind that perhaps he would be returned to the forest, returned to his home and family. However, it was not to be. The vehicle followed a different path, stopping finally in front of a large house. A distant memory flickered but vanished just as quickly at the sight of the human's building.

The man spoke to him in a constant, friendly stream of sounds that Shadow, of course, couldn't understand. He was led inside the door of the house. Strange sights and smells greeted his senses. The man led him through the house, down carpeted hallways and back again.

A small area containing many human items —long sticks with strange thick hair on one end —also contained two bowls similar to those from the shelter. These were filled with water and a pile of small meat-scented pellets. Food. In his mind, he found amusement at what these humans must think about what dogs preferred to eat.

After a thorough tour, the man unhooked his leash and let him explore on his own. Shadow did so. The scent of another dog still lingered in the area, an older one who was long gone. He took some small comfort in the fact that the scent contained no traces of fear or panic. The previous dog had been cared for and loved.

Shadow took in the feel of the place. He could sense that the man's pack also lived here, though they were not there at the moment. He guessed that he smelled the imprint of human cubs, fresh and floral, tinged with the energy of the young. He couldn't help but be curious about what sort of creatures these cubs might be. Did they live in nests, like the small birds he had observed in the forest? Did they romp and play, learning to fight and hunt as he and his pack mates had? He didn't have long to wait, however, because a burst of sudden words and laughter jolted him out of his thoughts.

A different human female and two human cubs bounded into the room. Shadow backed into the wall, despite his resolve to go along with everything. Another small pang erupted in his heart at the thought of Ula, lost to him now. She might know what to do with the human cubs. Perhaps she would even like them.

The adult humans greeted each other with a strange nuzzle, pressing their lips together briefly. Shadow barely noticed this because the two cubs had surrounded him, strange, smiling faces near his own. They jabbered in the language of humans. The newness of it all overcame him and he backed away, trying to become as small as he could. The man chastised his brood as they ran off, vanishing down a hallway toward another part of the house.

Shadow realized with some relief that, for the time being, he was now being left on his own. The human female opened the back door. A medium-sized white cat entered through the door, casting a sidelong glance at him as she did.

"Oh, hello," she purred as if she had been expecting him.

Shadow didn't reply.

"They have been speaking of you," she said. She drew her voice out in long relaxed sounds, pausing to lick her paw. "I expected they would eventually go back and fetch you."

"What is this place?" Shadow asked finally.

"Don't you know? This is your new home," the cat said with surprise. "You've been adopted."

Chapter Nine

The two adult humans sat down at the table, intently watching Shadow and the cat. Shadow paid no attention to them except to keep a level of alertness to their whereabouts, just as he would in the forest when faced with another forest creature that the pack had not yet marked for prey.

"Adopted?" Shadow said. "But I have a family, and I need to get back to them. How can I get out of this place?"

The cat sniffed with disdain. "I can come and go as I please. The backyard fence is of little consequence to me, but if Ginger was any indication, you won't be getting out of here. Not anytime soon."

"Why not?" Shadow said. He didn't like the tone of this cat, but if he could find a way to make her an ally, then he would do so. For now, he needed information. "And who is Ginger?"

"Ginger was the last dog," the cat explained. "Died about a month ago. Oh, don't worry. He died of old age. They took good care of him, it seemed. He was happy enough."

"And you?" Shadow pressed. "Are you happy?"

The cat turned toward him with a distant look, and seemed as if she might answer, but at that moment, the human-cubs returned to the room. The boy, by what Shadow could guess, was the smaller of the two. He walked over and began to pet him behind the ears, much in the way the human female had at the shelter. The feeling felt good, but Shadow didn't like that he enjoyed it. He wanted to remain distant from them because he didn't intend on being here long. He recalled something that he had seen the dogs do at the shelter when they approached the door. Perhaps he could copy the technique and make them open the door.

Shadow walked over to the back door, as the cat watched with amusement. He sat down and scratched the door with one paw. He let out a small, short yip. This seemed to impress the humans to no end as they exclaimed and vocalized in delight. The boy came over and with another scratch behind the ears, opened the door to the outside.

Shadow exited joyfully, only to find that the yard had a high wooden fence. The cat had mentioned that, after all, he remembered. Nonetheless, he circled the area, sniffing and exploring. At first, he found nothing that could be a weakness in the fencing. No matter, he would find a way out somehow.

The human cubs pulled out a basket of toys. There were balls of various sizes and a few small stuffed shapes that looked and smelled as if they had been chewed on by the previous dog. He took little interest in most of them, but responded with feigned enthusiasm when the ball was thrown. Finally, when he was panting and refused to chase the ball anymore, the family went back inside, leaving him alone with the cat.

"They're not so bad, really," the cat explained. "They mean well. They all do. Except for the ones who don't."

"What exactly does that mean?" Shadow asked.

"Humans," she explained. "They mean well."

"The human man stole me away from my family, from the forest. He did not mean well."

***

The following weeks, Shadow developed a routine with this new family.

He followed along when taken out on the leash, was led around the neighborhood for a short while and then returned back to the home. Sometimes, he was let inside during the night, but mostly, he and the cat were placed out the back door into the yard at the end of the day.

He learned that the cat's name was Clementine, and she kept him company. At least, as much as her distant aloofness could be called company; at other times, she would disappear over the edge of the fence with a dismissive flick of her tail.

He ate the dry, dead-tasting food they gave him and drank the water. He missed the forest and his family. A few more times, he attempted to reach out to them with his mind—at the very least to try and alert them to his presence—but to no avail. He determined that he had simply been taken too far away from the pack to reach them through the mind connection.

His melancholy mood was occasionally peppered with small bits of joy that Shadow begrudgingly allowed himself to feel: The sensation of having his ears scratched by the girl cub, rambunctious wrestling with the boy cub, the taste of the juicy tidbits that the girl-cub slipped to him under the table, and even the occasional conversation with Clementine. Once, the human woman had taken him into her lap and stroked him, but he was so confused by the warmth of it that he jumped down away from the gentle hand. He did not want to be ruled by the humans, even if they "meant well."

All of these pleasures of being a pet dog paled in comparison to the feeling he had gotten when running free with his pack mates in the forest. He missed the company of wolves. He missed their mind connections. He missed the hunts and the fresh-killed foods that came with the life of a wolf.

One night, both he and the cat had been allowed to stay inside. Clementine sat at the window, peering out at the rain streaming down the panes. Shadow curled up at the foot of the female human, who had in her lap a small paper object that she occasionally marked on with a little sliver of wood. He had seen her do that often and had no idea of the purpose of her motions. Clementine had explained that this was a game, but Shadow didn't know how that could be possible as it didn't involve running or tumbling of any kind.

The man human had vanished into another

room, which he often did in the evenings, Shadow had noticed. Sometimes, he spoke into a small box that he held at the side of his head, and got quite agitated as he did so at the voices that spewed into his ear. On this night, he had brought a small stack of papers out to the main area, and placed them on the large table. The man unfolded one of these papers until it nearly encompassed the whole surface. He worked silently, measuring and marking along different places on the large page.

The female human stood and disappeared down the hall, returning a moment later wearing her night garments. She gave the man a quick nuzzle and then vanished once more to their sleeping den. The man stayed, peering over the papers for a little while longer before he, too, disappeared down the same tunnel. He had left all of his work out on the table and Shadow wondered at that. Usually, the adults seemed very particular that the human-cubs should clean up after themselves and Shadow wondered why the man wouldn't do the same in turn.

"Do you want to see?" Clementine asked.

"See what?" Shadow said.

"The stuff," she said with a mischievous tone. "There is nothing more fun than walking all over human stuff when they are asleep," she said gleefully. The cat then hopped up onto the surface of the table, her steps making light crinkling sounds each time her paw came down. She circled the space, her eyes sparkling in delight with each movement. "Come and see," she invited again.

"You are not supposed to be up there, you know," Shadow said.

"Ooh." Clementine rolled her eyes. "The big, wild wolf dog is suddenly following the rules? Is it possible you have succumbed to domesticity?"

Shadow was already annoyed, but felt the barb was pushing the limit.

"I have not," he mumbled.

"Somebody's tame. Somebody's tame," she replied in a mocking sing-song voice, obviously taunting him.

"Fine!" he said at last. "I'll come and look if you stop bothering me!"

Clementine giggled as she watched Shadow hop carefully up onto one of the chairs, place his paws on the edge of the table and peer over the man's papers. He had not expected to see much, but instead, the view before him captivated his attention.

At first, the image on the large sheet of paper looked like nothing more than a misshapen blob, but the shape was immediately one that he knew. Back in the forest, when connecting with the other pack members in the midst of the hunt, he could almost see what the others could see. While he had run forward, deftly avoiding brambles and roots shooting out of the ground to trip his progress. He could also sense the sight of the Alpha, of Mother, of the quickness of his brother Thunder as he darted around tree trunks, of Storm eyeing the horizon as he pressed forward.

Each of these pieces of vision had linked together in such a way that he had known the shape of the forest, the curve of the creek bed. He knew where the trees ended and where each meadow began. He knew where the hard road ran, and what areas to avoid during hunting season. These shapes had become ingrained into his knowledge. He knew he would never forget the terrain of the place where he had lived with the wolf pack. So, he had no doubts when he peered down on the paper in front of him that the shape before him was a representation of the forest. *His forest.*

The line along the edge represented the road. Another wavier line echoed the flow of the creek. Certain gradated circles existed in the same place where the meadows would have been. Shadow peered closely, trying to make out the strange markings the human man had made on the page, but he couldn't make sense of it. Clementine seemed to sense his discomfort.

"What?" she asked, acknowledging his change in mood. "What is it? What's happened?"

"The forest," he said. "This is a picture of the forest where my pack lives."

"What's a 'pack'?" she asked.

"My family. Brothers and sisters. Mother and father. Others, too."

"All of you lived together?"

"Yes, in the forest."

"I can't even remember my mother. It's been so long since I was a kitten," Clementine said.

"That's what I'm afraid of. That I will lose… all that I knew of the wolves. All that I… *was* with them."

"I don't understand," she said to him.

"Yes, you do," Shadow said. "When you leave the yard and go over the fence on your own, do you not become what you once were? A hunter? A wild cat like a mountain lion? I know you hunt, Clementine. You come back smelling of birds on your breath. And of mice. Even, of moths. When you are out of their sight, you become more of what you are. What you and your kind once were." He paused. "That is the same for me. When I am free, I am myself. And when I am with my pack, we are more together than we are alone."

Clementine stared at him for a long while, as he kept his eyes on the large paper, almost as if trying to find a way to climb into the page and go back to his beloved home. Shadow had not always gotten along with the cat, but they were the only animals in this house and, as such, had formed somewhat of an alliance. Clementine had taught him the ways of how to get more food, how to get the humans to open the door when needed, and so on.

Shadow saw a series of squares that had been drawn in a different medium against the map of the forest. Symmetrical shapes that lined up neatly alongside each other. He didn't know what this represented, but he couldn't help but feel that somehow his family was in danger. After a long look at the forest that was represented on the paper, he climbed down from the table, knowing he had committed it all to memory.

Shadow recalled the first time he had seen the man in the forest.

The experience had startled him, of course. The man had not carried himself in the manner that the hunters did. Up to that point, he had only seen hunters in the distance, sometimes tracking the very same deer as the pack. But the man had then brought food, which had confused Shadow at the time because when animals in the pack brought food to each other, it meant they were connected.

Now, he realized that the man had tricked him with the food offering. Perhaps Shadow being vulnerable to humans had something to do with the difference between himself and the other wolves. A wolf would have never done it. A wolf would never have trusted a human and traded his freedom for a bit of food. When he realized what he had done and what he had set in motion—all for a bit of food—he realized what a serious mistake it had been to trust a human. A mistake so serious that it seemed that he might never see any of his pack again, or enjoy his freedom again, or know the wolf life again.

Shadow had seen his own reflection in standing pools of water when he had quenched his thirst with his wolf pack family. Now, he realized that, physically, at least, he more resembled the dogs he had seen at the shelter than the wolves he considered to be his brothers and sisters. He didn't know what to make of this new insight, but he did know one thing. He had to get back to the forest. He had to warn the others. Against what, he didn't know, but he knew they were in danger and he knew that he was the only one who could warn them.

"Okay, cat." He turned resolutely toward Clementine. "I need your help."

"Why?" The cat tilted her nose in the air. She had often listened to his tales of the forest and Shadow determined that she only half-believed them.

"Little cougar, you are the only one clever enough to help me." He hoped that his flattery would have an effect.

"Well," Clementine said, rubbing a paw over her ear. "I suppose that is true. What do you need help with?"

"When you go over the fence," he said, "what's on the other side?"

The cat gazed at him, carefully measuring her words. "Not much, really," she replied. "More grass. A few more houses. Birds, lots of birds." She licked her lips and burped a bit.

Shadow tried to maintain his patience. "Are there trees?" he pressed. "Is there any forest nearby? Big trees?"

Clementine thought. "I don't think so," she said finally. "I've roamed pretty far and all I know of this area is houses and yards. Sometimes, there are bicycles and mice, but no. I don't think we are close to any forest. There are small trees. I can jump down easily from the tops of them."

Shadow walked in a small circle. "If I could just get out of that backyard, then I could find the big trees. I could get oriented."

"Oriented to what?" Clementine asked.

"To find my way back," he said. "I'm always on that silly leash or trapped in the fenced yard. It's infuriating, really. Why do *you* get to come and go as you please?"

Clementine smirked. "I always come back. I don't have to, but I choose to. It allows for more freedom. If they opened the gate, they know you would not return."

"That is true. I would not. Do you know where the forest is?" Shadow asked.

"No," she said. "Just houses. Houses as far as I have ever roamed."

Shadow walked over to another part of the living room.

Clementine sat, cleaning one paw and then wandered into the kitchen. He heard the dry crunching sounds of her nibbling on her food. Food that smelled so vile that they didn't need to keep her bowl on the kitchen counter. There was no way he would ever eat a morsel of it.

He lay down, but his mind raced. Now more than ever, he knew he had to find a way back to his family. He didn't know how, but he had to find a way.

Chapter Ten

A few weeks later, Shadow got his chance.

Every day, he had examined the routines of this human family, the walks in the neighborhood, the time spent in the backyard. He had carefully examined the wall around the yard, looking for a space between the ground and the bottom of the fence, to no avail. His attempts at digging his way out were met by scolding and stones wedged into the holes he had dug, until the perimeter of the yard was lined with stones at the bottom of the fence. At that point, he'd given up trying to dig his way out.

Clementine had sat by him with amusement at his insistence on finding a way out. But at last, the day came. Clementine told Shadow that the family had planned a day at the park. She said they had cleaned out a basket that only came out when they planned to put food in it and eat at the park. The cat had developed a rudimentary understanding of their speech and habits and so, she was able to sometimes translate what she overheard, on a very limited scale.

Shadow still thought that the sounds the humans made resembled a staccato cackle, much like that of a teasing jaybird. The sound made him cringe but he had been able to determine some meaning when combining the body language with the tone and inflection sometimes applied when they spoke to him. But for the more important details, he relied on the cat's interpretations.

"The park is located in the middle of town," Clementine had said. "There's a path that leads into a small grove of woods. Not the same as your forest. Practically an island surrounded by buildings and houses. I know the place. Despite the isolation, there is a lot of land. You should be able to find a way to lose them, if that is your objective."

"It is," Shadow insisted.

The family loaded the car in the garage as Shadow observed from the kitchen. He had forced himself to behave in a more affectionate way for the last few days, calming them into an idea that he was beginning to adjust so that they would take him to the park with them.

Clementine had noticed that they were pleased with this new development. Finally, the female human came over and clipped his leash onto his collar and led him into the back of the large vehicle. He had plenty of space behind the seats where the human-cubs sat. He watched the houses slip past through the window as they headed down the road being stroked down his back by the young ones who called him something like "Lucky." He did not know what the word meant and if that was some name they had given him, he certainly would not answer to it.

A large basket of food sat close by, invading his sense of smell with the tempting aromas. If not for that, he could have picked up on the nuances coming through the vents of the vehicle to see if he could grasp onto a familiar scent from the land whizzing by then. He curled into a ball on the floor of the swaying vehicle to represent some semblance of patience. Once they arrived at the park, he hoped he would be able to orient himself a little better. His plan was to slip away and head for the big forest, once he knew where he was.

After a short drive, the vehicle pulled to a stop. They unloaded, setting things up at a table.

It seemed odd that a table was out in the middle of nature and that they should take their food for miles to eat it there.

The man human attached Shadow's leash to a small tree close to the table. Shadow lay down with his chin on his paws and waited. He watched the two small humans play at tossing a ball back and forth, playing in the nearby meadow.

The human mother set up the food along the table, the smell reminding Shadow how hungry he had become since his time with the family. The dry pellet food they provided him filled his belly, but he missed the thrill of the hunt and the reward of fresh meat shared with the pack. Again, he wondered where they were in that moment. Prior attempts to reach out with his mind and connect with the pack had yielded no results. He sat and waited. When the family finally sat down to eat, the man brought over Shadow's bowl, filled with the customary dry pellets. It was disappointing that they did not share their better meal with him.

When they finished and began to put the items away, the man walked over and took control of Shadow's leash. They headed down the paved path into the depths of the park. The path led to another path that had been cut through the trees.

This forest would have resembled Shadow's home terrain, were it not for the overwhelming scent of the humans that frequented this place. As they walked along, Shadow noticed the absence of creatures, whereas his woods had been teeming with birds, deer, elk and especially rabbits. All manner of creatures flying overhead and burrowing under the ground were in his forest. This forest had not much more than the few birds and squirrels that had become accustomed to the presence of the humans and begged for food from them.

The children moved ahead, sometimes running and leaping, but returning back to their parents with some interesting leaf or tree branch they had found. Shadow walked alongside the adults as they moved along the path at an annoyingly slow pace. The movement of the air gave Shadow the opportunity to figure out where he was. He lifted his nose as they walked along.

Surrounding them was the dry scent of earth and trees, intermingled with the overlay of the many humans who had traversed these paths recently—dozens, if not hundreds. But Shadow's sensitive nose reached beyond the immediate area, recognizing the oily scent of cars, exhaust and the city beyond the edges of the small forest-island in which they existed.

People, cars, buildings... He reached even further with his nose and with his mind.

The edges of the city couldn't be far, he hoped. He tried to shut out his mind to any other distractions to home in more completely on what he could smell.

And then... and *then*... beyond the cars beyond the buildings, his mind connected with a distant familiarity. The tiniest molecule of something familiar had traveled from one part of the world to another. Shadow recognized the scent, however small, of the distinctive pine-scented stands that surrounded the edges of the mountains through which he once roamed. The tree trunks far away were scented with something else. Wolf-marked tree trunks. He could smell them from a long distance.

Overjoyed, Shadow recognized the Alpha's scent on the wind. His heartbeat increased as he inhaled once more. He could picture almost exactly where he was at that moment, and how far away the forest was. If he could find a way to escape these humans, he could make it back. Back to Father, the Alpha, whose scent was available. And to Mother Wolf, who was almost always at his side.

Shadow hoped the wind wouldn't change. He needed to stay downwind of the scent he recognized and run into it with his nostrils flaring. He wished he were loose to turn his face into the wind and rush into the scent he knew and loved. The scent of the pack.

Shadow turned his head to look at the leash. The man walked trustingly, with the strap dangling loosely from his hand as he smiled and spoke with the female human. The human cubs had run up ahead and he could hear their laughter. Shadow examined the path around them. If he could pull the leash from the man's hand, he could cut through the woods. He already knew they wouldn't unhook the leash at any point during their visit. He had not earned the right to roam freely, he had determined.

A little bird chirped nearby, calling out a cheery song. Shadow weighed his options, and then made a sudden break for it.

The leash jerked through the man's fingers as Shadow pulled with a quick side-step into the forest. Immediately, both grown humans began to shout something at him and he realized it was the name they had given him. Not his real name and he would not be recalled by it.

At first, his goal was to get as much distance between himself and the humans as he could. But immediately, he realized that he had to get the leash off of him. The offending strap dragged along behind him, snagging on branches and pulling along the leaves on the ground. But

Shadow moved forward in a mad dash to put distance between himself and the human family who had fed him and petted him and played with him. It was not enough to win his loyalty, though. After all, the human man had stolen him from his family and nothing could ever make up for that.

As he ran, he could hear the shouts of the humans calling after him.

The girl, who had sometimes dressed him in clothing and tied ribbons in his fur, had begun to cry, which made Shadow feel a slight pang, but he kept running. The handle of the leash snagged on a broken edge of a tree that jutted out of the ground. The leash pulled him back by his neck while the velocity whipped him around backward. He scrambled his feet and dug in his heels, pulling backward until his head popped free of the collar with a painful snap that crunched past the cartilage of his ears. With some surprise, Shadow realized he had broken free and could now run unencumbered.

Should have tried that ages ago, he thought.

Shadow ran onward, trees and earth whipping past in a blur as he ran the fastest he ever had. Now that he had a plan, he felt a new rush of adrenaline surge through him. He ran onward, his senses becoming heightened as he did so. Up ahead was the busy road that ran alongside the park. He would have to avoid this but maybe go along and find a way to cross all of the lines of machines that the cat had told him were called 'cars.'

He had one little pang for Clementine the cat, whom he would never see again. But she was half-free and was allowed to roam and chose to return to her easy life with the humans. Where nothing was ever expected of her. Nothing.

It was different for him. And he knew what he wanted and who he wanted. He just had to get home and then everything would be the same as it once was.

Shadow knew that if he followed along the large road, he might come across the road that would lead him back to the forest. His forest, not this park that was made by human hands, but one that grew naturally. He slowed his pace when he realized that the family behind him had turned back and were leaving without him.

They had stopped their shouting and pursuit and would no doubt return to the car. The car! He had not thought about that. If they did so, they might come along the freeway and see him running along the edge of the hard road. He would have to find another way.

The little bird that had sung so happily had followed him when he'd run from the humans.

He turned toward it, watching it hop from branch to branch, sailing alongside him with wings outstretched.

"Where are you going?" he chirped.

Shadow regarded the little creature. Though small, he recognized that this bird had lived in freedom his whole life. Always able to fly to his heart's content, hunting bugs and seeds in his own way, making his own life in the treetops.

"I'm going home," Shadow explained.

"Where is home, Dog Who Thinks He's a Wolf?" the bird asked with a happy swoop of his wings.

Shadow smiled at the name the bird had given him. "I'm going back to the forest to find my pack. My family."

"Of course," the bird said in his sing-song voice. Suddenly, Shadow had an idea.

"Do you ever go to the forest?" he asked the bird.

"This forest?" the bird said, sweeping his wings around to indicate the surroundings.

"No," Shadow explained. "The big forest. Where the wolves live. My wolves."

The bird eyed him with a twinkle of mischief. "I go there sometimes. If the worms are hiding in this park."

"I see," said Shadow. "So, you know the way?"

"To the wolves' forest? Yes," said the bird.

"Can you go there?" Shadow asked. "If I give you a message, can you find the wolf pack that lives at the base of the mountains by the lake? Can you find that place?"

Shadow asked with such sincerity that the little bird couldn't help but be moved by his plea. He agreed, and Shadow described to him what they looked like. He was unsure if they still remained in the same grove as he remembered, but he was certain that they wouldn't have gone far.

"There is danger coming to the pack. Explain to them that I have seen something in the house of the man who took me. A picture depicting the forest in which they live. Tell them there is danger and they should travel up the mountain to safety."

"What kind of danger?" the bird asked.

"I don't know," Shadow said. "The humans are bringing something different to the forest. I think they mean to change the land in a way that wolves cannot live there any longer."

"The humans?" The little bird let out a trill of laughter. "They are not dangerous. They bring grains and food to throw on the ground when food is scarce. They wouldn't harm the forest."

"Please," Shadow said to the bird with a tiny

voice. "Can you just deliver the message?"

"I can," the bird said.

"Thank you." Shadow heard a rustle in the forest behind them. "And tell them I am coming. I will meet them in the mountains, once I make my way home."

The bird flew away, disappearing into the sky as a little dot against the expanse of sky.

Shadow turned back to make his way closer to the edge of the park. Once he spied the many lines of cars ahead of him, he stayed hidden in the shadows of the trees. He would have to avoid humans and cars as much as possible until he could get to the part of the land that was uninhabited by humans or traveled by cars.

He pressed forward. The sky darkened as the sun passed behind a cloud. Much to his dismay, raindrops begin to fall. Shadow had come to the edge of the park and up ahead, he sensed the smells wafting from the buildings. It was human food, but food, nonetheless.

He wanted to find shelter and think through which path he should take through town to reach the outer edges without harm. The many lines of cars veered off in another direction and the smaller hard road in front of him was not as wide, with far fewer cars. Shadow trotted across the road between a pause in the traffic. He didn't see many humans around and the ones he did see paid no attention to him.

Down a little alley, Shadow found shelter from the rain, nothing more than an awning over a hard pavement. But next to that was a large Dumpster. Piles of cardboard boxes had been spilled out, which contained the real reason for him finding shelter here.

While waiting for the rain to subside, Shadow dragged one of the boxes open to find a whole pizza, covered in cheese and some kind of sliced meat. He ate it and found it to be quite delicious, like nothing he had eaten before. With a full stomach and a warm enclosure to hide in, the strum of the rain against the metal awning lulled Shadow into sleepiness.

He had much to think about, but for now, he would simply take a quick nap.

Chapter Eleven

Shadow awoke to the sound of canine voices nearby. Gruff voices. There were three dogs of various breeds. And obviously, he was trespassing on their territory.

The sun slanted at an angle into the alley that let him know several hours had passed. *How long had I been asleep?* he wondered. He opened his eyes, careful not to move and reveal his wakefulness. They spoke in hushed whispers, and he listened for a little while.

"What should we do with him?" one said.

"What do you mean, *do*? We can't do anything with him. He's just another dog. He'll go his own way when he wakes up."

"But you know, what if *she* finds out?"

"If we get him to move on, she won't find out."

"But he's found our stash. How do we know he doesn't know about the other places?"

"The other places haven't been compromised. None of the food is missing, except one pepperoni pizza."

"But what if we don't know the other food is missing?"

"Shh! I think he's waking up."

Shadow thought he had been as still as he could while they spoke and he felt unsure how he might have revealed himself. He slowly lifted his head and turned to face them.

He saw three dogs, just as he had thought. One larger dog had long, reddish coarse fur drooping around his face like a white mustache. The other dog was mid-sized with short brown hair and one ear flopped over. The third had about the same build as the short hair but with a beautiful golden, shaggy coat. All three were covered in a thin layer of dust and city grime. Shadow wondered how long they had been on their own, and thought, momentarily, about taking a dip in the calm part of the stream in the forest when he got back.

The large dog turned toward Shadow.

"It's all right," he said. "Come forward."

Shadow stood, shook himself awake and

walked to the small group. He had no intention of tarrying in any way with them. He had apparently slept the evening away and needed to get back to the forest.

"What's your name?" the large reddish dog asked.

Shadow simply looked at him, his gaze never wavering.

"I'm sorry," the dog said. "My name is Red. This is Switch. The fluffy one is Goldie. We're waiting for the She-Alpha. She told us to meet her here after our hunting for the day."

Switch nudged him quietly, giving Red a look that clearly indicated he thought he'd said too much.

Shadow eyed them with caution. What he described sounded a great deal like the instructions that had been given to them by Mother back in the forest, when they were given leave to hunt, as long as they returned within a certain time. Shadow had found a box of pizza, so perhaps these dogs knew of more places in the city much like this one. Places where food may be more plentiful, just like he knew of in the forest.

The yellow dog, Goldie, spoke next. "She-Alpha will decide what to do with you. You've walked onto our turf, you see. And helped yourself to one of our pizzas."

"I didn't know it was yours. And I'd like to keep walking," Shadow said. "If it's all the same to you, I'm trying to get to the forest. I have no desire to stay. Your turf can remain undisturbed."

"That's all fine and good," Goldie continued, "but you see, you've eaten one of our pizzas. So, how do we know you aren't one of the Mulligan Gang?"

"The what?" Shadow said. What on earth had he walked into?

The large dog, the one who had called himself Red, stepped forward, giving Goldie a sideways glance. "There's no need for overreacting," he said. "When She-Alpha gets here..."

"Um, guys," Switch spoke for the first time. All three of them looked past Shadow and lowered their heads.

Shadow turned to see their She-Alpha walking in silhouette down the alley, the yellow glow of the setting sun behind her. She looked smaller than Shadow had assumed she would be, but soon, her shape became more familiar as she neared. She stepped into the light, revealing a shaggy, dirty black and white coat. Out of the corner of his eye, he saw the other three lowering their heads in a sign of respect for their leader. The female Alpha dog glanced over them and let her gaze fall on Shadow, who looked at her with astonishment.

"Ula, is that you? All grown up?"

"Hi, Shadow," she replied with a tail wag and a tongue loll. "I see you've met the boys."

Chapter Twelve

After a greeting of circles, yipping and nose touching, while the other three looked on with amazement, the group of dogs sat around the warmth of a kitchen vent. They gnawed on some stale crusts, while Ula told Shadow what had transpired since she had last seen him in the shelter.

"After you left the shelter," Ula said, "I got adopted. No one believed me when I told them you were a feral dog. That sort of thing isn't seen very often. But I stuck to what you had told me. I could read in your mind that it was true. I never doubted it. Needless to say, that made me a bit of a target at the shelter."

"Yes," Shadow said. "But what else happened with you? How did you get here?"

"I was adopted by a young couple. They seemed nice at first. They came into the shelter and looked over several dogs before settling on me. Something struck me as odd about them, though. Instead of taking any of us to the playroom or the courtyard, these people picked me up, felt up and down my legs, and watched how I walked. That sort of thing. The humans at the shelter apparently didn't find anything strange about their behavior because they adopted me out to them. I was so excited to finally have a home. But I soon learned the reason for the strange examination at the shelter, and the dream of my happy home was not meant to be."

"What was it?" Shadow asked, looking at the many scars that showed through her fur and her torn, healed ears. "What happened to you?"

"They took me to a place with other dogs, a large warehouse. The whole place reeked of fear and blood. I was terrified. First, they shaved off all of my fur. Then, I was tied to a leash at the end of a long pole and other dogs were brought in to me. Aggressive, mean dogs. It soon became clear that my role was for the other dogs to unleash their aggression on me before being put into a pit to fight each other. Sort of warming up for their fights."

Shadow listened with horror. He had never

heard of such an atrocity. "I don't understand. Why? Why would they do this horrible thing to you?"

"For sport. They called me a bait dog," Ula continued. "The first few weeks were terrible. I was kept in a small enclosure, unable to escape as the other dogs built up their killer instincts before they were forced to fight each other. I tried to talk to them at first, like I am talking to you right now, but I realized these dogs had something wrong with them. Their minds were not right, as if they had been bred and trained for this terrible hatred and came out of this training with a fever for fighting. I thought I would die from my many wounds. I was no match for any of them. They were all larger than me. And all of them were bent on murder."

"How did you escape?" Shadow asked, shocked at what Ula was telling him.

"Finally, one day, a new dog had been put in with me. Bigger, meaner. That had been an especially hard time, up to that point. I truly feared for my life at every moment. A large, muscular dog stepped toward me—his head was almost as wide as his shoulders. His eyes were looking right through me and his mouth was already bloody. Foam dripped from his mouth as if he had eaten something he shouldn't have. As usual, he was goaded into attacking me—the humans poked him with sticks and shouted at him until he became even more agitated. I often came out of these situations nothing more than a bloody pulp, wondering from one day to the next when I would be killed."

"Oh, Ula. I am so sorry." He nodded for her to go on.

"That day, I presumed, would be no different. As soon as he appeared, I could see the rolling whites of his eyes, the flash of his teeth. In the past, I had tried to be submissive, in hopes that the other dog would show mercy. This never worked. Keep in mind that I never once blamed the other dogs. They were victims, just as I was. Whatever these people had done to them was a terrible, terrible thing. But despite this, I soon realized that I had to find a way to survive. This dog before me was terrified, too, I could see, but he wasn't terrified of me."

"He was terrified of them, the humans," Shadow said.

"Yes. So, I tried something I had never thought of before."

"You fought back," Shadow guessed.

"Yes.

I held up my head and looked him straight in the eye. When he lunged at me, I dodged and snapped back. I had never done this before. It goes against my nature. Immediately, I heard the humans react to my self-defense moves. They all began to gather around and chant something. I pushed myself into dominance. Remembering how the dogs in the shelter had tried to dominate each other, I did that, too. I didn't want to hurt the other dog, but he kept coming at me, again and again, ripping up my flesh. Finally, I ducked under him and pretended I was going to show my belly, but instead, I latched onto his throat and brought him down to the ground."

Shadow nodded for her to go on.

"I knew if I let him up, I would die. So, I didn't let him up. I had his throat in my tightest grip and he fought and fought, never giving up. I squeezed his throat to keep him down and soon, he... died." She paused. "I didn't mean it to go that far, but if I would have let him up, it would have meant my own death. So, I chose life."

Shadow was shocked. Ula, the happy-go-lucky dog from the shelter, had killed another dog. He didn't know what to say. Not even in his wolf pack had one of his family ever killed another member. It would be unthinkable.

"It was self-defense," he said to comfort her.

"Shadow, I didn't want to do it, but I had to. When you see that the end is coming for you, you will do anything to survive. All I could think was, 'How can I get out of this alive?'"

Shadow and the others bowed their heads to her, in respect and awe of what she had done to save her own life.

"What happened when the other dog died?" Shadow asked.

Ula said, "Since I was just the bait dog and very injured, the humans didn't want to put me in the ring to fight, but they also knew they couldn't have me injuring the fighting dogs. I think they thought it was a fluke because they kept me on as a bait dog for a little while, still bringing dogs to me to excite them as easy prey before they put them in the real fighting pit. But word got around that the bait dog had had enough. That a mere female dog was showing her will to survive. That was how I learned to become an Alpha."

"You earned it," Shadow said.

"I did. Soon, no dog would even come at me, not even the biggest ones. Even with the strange things that the humans had done to them, going against an Alpha goes against any dog's nature. And I was, and am, an Alpha."

She glanced toward the pack around her with a wry glance as they all tucked their heads down. Shadow noticed a small smile exchanged between all of them and immediately knew that the dynamic between Ula and her pack was that she ruled them. He turned back to her to hear the rest of the story.

Ula continued, "It became clear that I no longer would function as a bait dog as the fighters always came away bloodied now, and were unable to effectively fight in the real fighting pit. I was no longer the warm-up dog. And to the humans, that meant only one thing."

"Did they abandon you?" Shadow asked.

"Oh no. I would have loved to be put on the street to run away. They intended to put me down. I could smell the intentions of the man with the gun who took me out to the forest that day."

Shadow had seen the human hunters and what he now knew were called guns. He had seen how they could make a killing happen, even from a distance with the strange method that produced such a loud sound and felled even the largest of creatures in the forest. The deer, the elk, the bear. All had fallen to the sound that cracked through the forest from a stick pointed by humans at an animal. Not a stick. A gun. Shadow had yet to understand how it worked, but he knew that all of the animals he knew feared this weapon.

"Where did he stop with you?"

"He didn't take me far, just outside the city," Ula said. "Once we got out into the trees, he dragged me, snapping and snarling, into the cover of the shadows on the leash, to hide from anyone nearby what he was doing. I sensed his gun on his hip, smelled it. I knew if I pulled loose and ran, he would point the gun at me and fell me with the sound it makes."

"What did you do?" Shadow asked.

"I turned on him. Barking and snarling, I turned loose every bit of resentment and hatred inside of me for what he had done to me. How he had used me. How he had taken away my life without killing me. And I fought for the others, too, even the ones who used me as a bait dog. It was what they were trained to do. And I fought for the other bait dogs, most of whom had died."

She paused, remembering, her eyes far away. "My aggressive plan worked. He backed away, scrambling to reach for his metal stick, but I snapped at his hands until he had to hold them over his head to escape being bitten. He ran back to the truck, abandoning me—then and there."

"And then what?" Shadow asked, his heart pounding.

"He sped off, leaving me free to roam and most importantly, leaving me alive. I had only known the city at that time. I knew I couldn't survive in the woods by myself, so I found my way back to the city."

"I want to leave the city so badly and just as badly, you wanted to find it again," Shadow said in wonder.

"You have your way to survive and I have mine," she said simply.

"When she found the city again is when she found us," Goldie interjected. "I pulled the dragging leash from her neck."

"And I chewed off her collar and the dangling muzzle," Red said.

"That is true," Ula said. "I stumbled across one of their food stashes. Not here." She gestured with her nose toward the pile of pizza boxes behind them. "I think it may have been Mao's China Hut, three blocks over."

"Yeah, that's right," Red confirmed. "I remember because you took all of the sesame chicken."

Ula laughed. "I had to prove a point… that a female dog can be an Alpha."

"Fair enough," Red said.

"But I don't understand," Shadow said after mulling over the story for a moment. "How did Ula become your leader?"

"She's an Alpha." Switch spoke this time. "A dog can't really go against that. She is not the largest of us, but she is the wisest and the fiercest."

"That's true," Shadow agreed. "Does it work the same for a dog pack as it does for a wolf pack?"

Ula said, "From what you told me, yes. I think so."

"Speaking of the forest," Shadow said, "I have to go. I have lost track of time. If the bird delivered my message to the pack, they'll be expecting me. And if they are on the move, I have to find out where they went before snow or rain covers up their tracks."

"Go?" Switch said. "You can't go. We need your help."

"Help with what?" Shadow asked.

"The Mulligan Gang," Red said. "Before Ula showed up, we thought you might have been one of them."

"What's the Mulligan Gang?"

Ula jumped in with the explanation. "Another dog pack is named after the man who once owned them. The story goes that he went away and did not return. His dogs got loose and escaped the dog catcher's noose. You see, we roam on this side of town. We stick to the shadows and alleys. We know what restaurants put out what food in the trash and what time of day they do it. It's a pretty decent life, actually. We just have to avoid the dog catchers and even the well-meaning humans who try to pick us up.

They try to lure us into their cars with bags of hamburgers."

"I will never take food from the hand of a human again," Shadow said. "Not even a human cub."

"We know better than that now," Ula said. "Look where that got me the first time. From a shelter to bait dog was nothing I ever expected when I willingly went with a woman who fed me from her hand when me and my littermates were put on the street to survive. And then she took me in her car to the shelter. Now, we have learned and come far. Now, we fight for turf, for territory. Now, we fight for survival."

Shadow listened carefully. His brief experience as an adopted pet had been easy, compared to hers. Except for the fact that he had never truly belonged to a human pack and never wanted to, he had not been so terribly mistreated. Not like Ula had. He shuddered to think of all she had been through since he had last seen her.

"This experience has changed you forever," he said softly.

"The choice was to change myself or die," she said. "Now, we always stay on this side of the city. The Mulligan Gang is the other pack that roams the other side of the city. The problem is that there is a small strip, just a few city blocks away, which falls under debate as to which pack will claim that area. It has a few choice restaurants. The steakhouse, for one. Prime eating. No pun intended."

"What will you do?" Shadow asked. "How will you figure out the territory?" He already knew the answer before she gave it because he knew what happened when a wolf pack crossed into another wolf pack's hunting territory.

Ula looked around at the dog pack. "We'll have a face-off with them in a day's time. Problem is, they outnumber us. There are four of us and six of them. If we had more dogs in our pack, we would stand a fighting chance. If you were with us, it would at least give us a chance to win. I do have a bit of a reputation as the dog who survived the fighting pit, but my experience only goes so far. I am small, compared to our enemies."

"I don't know," Red said. "You can be pretty intimidating when you want to be. Size is a factor, but not the only factor. You have courage and you are swift and ruthless when you have to be."

"Absolutely," Goldie said as he and Switch both nodded in agreement.

"Stop kissing up to me, boys," Ula said with an eye roll, but Shadow noticed again the small grin and chiding tone she used. She turned back to Shadow. "The truth is, Shadow, we need that territory. It has the only two steakhouses in the city. We're dogs. We can only survive on pizza crusts and sesame chicken for so long before we start going a little batty. We need meat. Bones. Fat scraps."

Shadow thought about it. He wanted to get back home to the forest. To meat, to bones, to fat scraps. And to his brothers and sisters and parents. That much was certain. But Ula had been the only friend he'd had in that horrible animal shelter. The advice she had given him had helped him survive, even after he had left with the human family with a leash and collar around his neck. He came to a decision. "Yes," he said. "I'll help you tomorrow. But I need to ask a favor in return."

"Anything at all," Ula said.

"The family I was with," Shadow explained. "The man has a picture of the forest, the same place where I lived with the wolf pack. I am not sure what it means exactly, but I am certain that my family is in danger. If they got the message I sent, they should leave the area. But if I can somehow stop the man, then we would have our home back."

"How would you stop him?" she asked.

"I don't know. I would get all of my wolf brothers and sisters together to—"

"To what?" Ula said. "You can't stop humans from doing what they want. They have cars and guns and leashes and muzzles. You can only run from them now, Shadow. The wolf pack must run, too. That is the only answer."

He considered her wise words. "You're right. If I help you win this territory in tomorrow's fight, will you help me get back home?"

"Of course," Ula said. "I will go with you as far as I can."

"Did you really grow up with a wolf pack?" Switch asked, his eyes wide with wonder.

"Yes, I did," Shadow said. He realized that for the first time, more than one dog believed him. A feeling of pride and sorrow washed over him as he thought about his wolf family and all he had learned from them and also, since leaving them.

"Tell us about it," Goldie said with a similar look of marvel.

Shadow glanced at Ula, who nodded her approval. They had many hours before dawn would come. The dogs settled in while Shadow regaled them with stories of his youth, beginning with Mother Wolf, who had defended him as fiercely and proudly as one of her own pups. And he told them of each of his wolf siblings, whom he considered his real brothers and sisters. They listened as he described the feeling of taking down prey with the single mindset of the pack working together in perfect harmony. He recalled for them the beauty of the untouched forest, the majesty of the mountains marking the edge of the forest, and the serene silver lake where the animals gathered for water and refreshment. Eventually, one by one, the dogs drifted off to sleep, each dreaming about running through the trees, feeling the freedom of the wind whipping through their fur as they plunged forward toward the horizon.

Shadow stayed awake for a long while, watching over his sleeping friends… like an Alpha would. It had been a long time since he had been part of a pack. It felt strange that they were not his family from the forest, but in their own way, he knew they were a family to each other.

Shadow knew that he was a dog but not a dog. He also knew that he was a wolf but not a wolf. Perhaps there was no one else like him. He lived between two worlds and now, he could choose where he wanted to be. It occurred to him that in a dog pack, he had a fair chance of becoming an Alpha. But in a wolf pack, he would not become an Alpha. He thought about his choices for a long time.

After the fight with the Mulligan Gang, he would go his own way, back to the wolf pack.

This, he decided.

He looked at Ula, over whose sleep he watched. It would be very hard to leave her. But his heart was in the forest with a wolf pack. Not here with a dog pack. He knew in his mind what he was physically… a dog of unknown parentage. But in his heart and mind, he was pure wolf.

He heaved a sigh as, try as he would, he could not stay awake another moment. He finally succumbed to dreams of running in the forest and someday, taking down an elk on his own. They were big dreams, as big and bold as he had ever had.

Chapter Thirteen

The dawn greeted the sleeping dogs, casting its golden glow over them.

Shadow opened his eyes first, noticing Ula had leaned her back against his during the night. He took comfort in the contact, as it reminded him of the feeling he had once enjoyed while curled up with his pack mates, back in the forest. It always came back to that. *The forest.*

When he shifted his weight, Ula stirred, opening one eye. She blinked once or twice and stood, stretching out her paws in front of her.

Shadow stood and wandered away for several moments to find a shadowed corner.

Ula began to nudge the other dogs with her nose to rouse them. Goldie woke up, followed by Switch. Ula had to tug on Red's ear to get his attention, but finally, he roused with a sleepy yawn.

"Time to wake up and look alert, boys," Ula said. "Today, we claim our territory from the Mulligan Gang."

"Shouldn't we eat first?" Red suggested with a sleepy grin.

"No." Shadow stepped back into the light. "If we fight—if it comes to that—we fight hungry. We run at them with fire in our eyes and with nothing to slow us down."

Ula turned, nodding her head to Shadow.

"What difference does it make?" Goldie asked. "Seems like we need to have our strength going into it."

"We'll eat afterward," Shadow said. His experience had taught him that the hunger made for a keener hunter. Ula knew as much, too.

The three dogs looked toward Ula for final confirmation.

"He is one of the wolf pack. He's seen things we couldn't even imagine," Ula said. "We will defer to him for this fight. He knows what he is talking about."

The five dogs walked in a line, keeping to the shadows that were still plentiful in the early light of morning. Shadow considered the small makeshift pack of which he had now become an important part. He had awakened feeling that he was almost home, even though he wasn't. And he realized it was because he was, again, part of a canine family, even if it would only be for a day. Though he didn't relish the idea of fighting another pack of dogs, he looked forward to the wildness, the sheer unpredictability of life on his own—and then, after he helped Ula's pack, he would depart for the forest, for the mountains, and not look back. This, he knew to be true with every wolf howl he had ever aimed at the sky.

They walked onward toward the territory overlap area, with Ula leading the way. After turning the corner toward the bare lot where they expected to meet the Mulligan dog pack, Ula dropped back to pace alongside Shadow.

"The others have never been part of a confrontation before," she said, only loud enough for him to hear. He understood what she meant. Red was an older dog, and his senses wouldn't be what they once were. Goldie and Switch, he sensed, had plenty of confidence, but he had seen how easily they deferred to Ula. It wouldn't take much for them to give into their submissive natures against the other dogs and go belly up. Ula sensed what he was thinking and nodded. "We need you, Shadow. We need your wolf instincts in this fight."

"But Ula," he whispered, "I'm not a wolf. As gracious as you have been, I am but a dog with a wolf's mind."

She nudged him with her snout, playful but serious. "You are more wolf than any of us," she said. "The dogs cannot beat us with you as leader of this fight."

Shadow did not know how to tell Ula this, but other than minor scraps in his wolf pack to establish the order of dominance, he had never really fought another canine, not at this level, which could be a fight to the death. And Ula... *had*.

They rounded the corner to the vacant lot. The building on one side cast a long shadow across the grassy plot and a chain-link fence ran along the other side.

Shadow examined the area and sized it up within seconds. They saw the other dogs across the way, sitting along the edge of the lot. Young dogs, all of them. Too young, Shadow determined. They exuded confidence and authority. That would be their downfall, Shadow determined, because in a fight, they would not fight as a pack, but as individuals. His experience in the forest had taught him that above all else, overconfidence would often be the downfall. As would a lack of discipline.

They took their places on the near side of

the lot. Goldie to his left. Ula next to Shadow. Switch and Red on the other side of their leader. Shadow sensed in Ula a heightened awareness, her senses honed and reflexes sharp to any surprises. He had no doubt that she had learned how to fight during her time as a bait dog.

The other Alpha stepped forward, a mangy shepherd with steely yellow eyes. "I see you have added to your ranks," he called across to Ula.

"I see your ranks remain the same, Brick," Ula said, calling him by name and matching his tone as she stepped forward.

Shadow could tell that she was flaunting her influence at having another member join the pack. *What they don't know can't hurt us*, he thought to himself.

Ula and Brick walked forward and began to slowly circle each other, throwing taunts.

"So, where did you find this guy with the curly hair?" Brick asked. "Is this overgrown poodle mutt one of your shelter dogs?"

Shadow cringed. Was that what he really was? He'd really no idea, despite the curly hair, and now, an enemy had just told him what he probably was.

"Pampered and spoiled like the others of his kind, I bet." Brick continued his taunting.

"You wouldn't believe me if I told you,"

Ula said. "I wouldn't underestimate him."

"And why not?" Brick circled her with stiffened legs and the hair up on the back of his neck. "He's not much more than any of the others. An old man, two boys and a She-Alpha. My guys are lean. They have reason to fight."

"It doesn't have to come to a fight," Ula said.

"Why shouldn't it?" the other shepherd said with a sneer.

"Because, he's Shadow," Ula said.

Shadow was surprised when the shepherd recoiled at the name, glancing back at the others who reacted in a similar fashion.

"Shadow, the wolf dog?" one of Brick's pack mates asked with disbelief dripping from his voice. "This mop is the feral dog that should have us trembling in our tracks?"

Shadow could smell the adrenaline spike that coursed through them. *Fear.*

Brick growled a warning over his shoulder, trying to rally the pack to keep up the show of strength.

They've heard of me, Shadow thought with some surprise. *But what have they heard?* He remained silent to see what would happen next.

"Enough talk," the shepherd said. "I don't care if you have the entire forest's wolf population at your beck and call! That territory behind the steak house is ours!" With that, he lunged at Ula. The shepherd had a clear size advantage over Ula, but she'd predicted his lunge and dodged beneath him, skittering beneath his feet as his teeth snapped together on thin air.

At the cue of the leaders, all of the other dogs tore across the lot, clashing into each other.

Shadow dove toward Brick, knocking him off his feet as Shadow crashed against his side like a mountain goat. Dust kicked up as the fighting rose up all around. Brick quickly regained his footing and turned back toward Shadow.

Ula was momentarily forgotten as Shadow's attention turned toward his new foe. Shadow's mind connected with ease with the other pack members and he directed them with a mind link. He sensed Red holding his own against the two smaller dogs. Goldie had one by the throat already and, against his gentler golden retriever nature, he was fighting for the right of his pack to feed in this prime territory.

Ula had circled around to draw one of the others off of Red, who seemed to be having a bit of trouble. Switch leaped at the heels of the other, dodging and diving against the snapping jaws. Very suddenly, Shadow flipped the other

Alpha on his back, just like he'd taken down prey as part of a pack. The idea was always to get the prey off their feet.

Shadow had managed to get the other dog's shoulders to the ground, forcing him to roll over in a submissive position. He held him there, snarling, but not wanting to fight to the death. That was it. The battle had been won before any serious damage had been done to either side. As in wolf pack battles, once either Alpha was down, the fight should end quickly.

Brick's eyes flashed in anger, even as his rollover admitted his defeat.

For another moment, Shadow stood over him snarling, then stepped back to let the dog retreat.

Brick slunk away to the other side of the lot. Seeing their leader admit defeat made the rest of the rival pack pull back, gathering behind him, their tails low and their spirits broken to the point where their heads hung almost to the ground.

Ula stepped forward to the middle of the lot with her head up and her chest out.

"Keep walking away, Brick, and take your friends with you," she said. "This territory is ours now."

The shepherd tossed his head toward them and Ula stood her ground, even as blood flowed from a wound. "Looks like you took a hit or two."

As the other dogs disappeared down the street, Ula turned toward Shadow. Goldie and Switch stood alongside him, gazing toward Red, who lay prone on a patch of dry grass.

Ula and Shadow rushed to his side. Shadow saw an ugly gash along Red's side where he lay bleeding profusely.

"Oh, no," Goldie whispered from behind them as they stepped closer.

"Don't worry," Ula told Red. "If we can get you to the alley, you'll be all right."

Red lifted his head, wincing at the movement. "I'm not going anywhere," he said, his voice a thin rasp. "Just to sleep and never wake again."

"Nonsense, Red," Ula said. She pressed her nose against his side, trying to nudge him. "Get up while you can."

"Ula, stop," he said, pulling from a strength he had once had. "I've been an Alpha, too, you know. You must defer to me this time."

"You were an Alpha?" Ula said.

"Yes," Red said. "But you already knew that, didn't you?"

Ula nodded.

"You've been a good leader, Ula," Red said. "And Shadow, having you in the pack made me feel like I was running through the woods again, just as I did as a young dog. Thank you both for that." He turned his attention back to Ula. "Now, listen. We made this dog a promise. It's time to get him home to the forest. To his wolf pack."

"Of course, Red," Ula said.

Red said to Shadow, "You showed me that you *are* a wolf. You fought today like a wolf. Don't ever let anyone tell you differently. Okay? You promise?"

"Okay," Shadow said, his voice thick. "I promise."

"You better," Red said. "Now, didn't we just win the territory? What are you hanging around here for? Go get some of that steak and..." They saw his eyes go dark.

"Red is gone," Ula said. "He was a good dog. A good friend."

Goldie and Switch both lay on either side of him, laying their heads alongside his. Ula stood over him, in a guarding stance. Not a one of them went for the steak bones in the trash barrels outside the back of the steakhouse.

Shadow did the only thing he knew to do at a time like this. He stood in front of Red and uttered a low, mournful howl that rose into the sky, giving a voice to all of their grief.

***

A few hours later, they returned from the alley behind the steak house, their bellies full from the restaurant's leavings of the night before. The meal had been tasty and well-earned, but the passing of Red had cast a solemn mood over all of them.

Shadow knew that the next goal would be to return to his wolf pack family. Ula's pack was diminished now, and weakened. He longed to see his own family again, but the idea of leaving his new friends at a definite disadvantage against another possible tangle with the Mulligan dog pack made him feel a sense of sadness and regret that he couldn't quite define. He had never felt loyalty to anyone, other than to his own pack. The bond he had with Snow, Chase, and Blue couldn't and wouldn't ever be replicated. But he glanced around at Goldie, Switch—and especially Ula—and found that he had formed a different kind of bond with them. They had become a pack, all different breeds, but they had come together, able to share the mind link in much the same way that he had with his own wolf pack.

"Deep thoughts?" Ula asked.

"It's going to be a big day," he said. "We have a long way to go to the forest."

Ula nodded and they silently walked along.

The city had awakened and more humans appeared here and there, prompting the dogs to stay even more toward the shadows. They headed toward the edge of the city. Finally, Shadow had been able to orient himself and knew which path would lead them to his grove.

Ula and the others would accompany him as far as the forest's edge, but at that time, he would insist that they turn back. They were city dogs and he didn't want to subject them to the dangers of the forest. Especially Ula, though perhaps she could more than hold her own here. But he didn't know if the wolf pack would accept his dog friends and let them interact in a friendly way. He doubted it.

Ahead, he saw a bend in the road. He knew that beyond it, the houses would thin out and eventually disappear altogether. Beyond that, he saw the green expanse of the forest, rising up the side of the mountain. He lifted his head to take in the welcoming scent. They walked onward, and Shadow's heart swelled with more hope with each step. Finally, they came to the small clearing alongside the road. They had been walking for a long while and the sun was directly overhead.

Shadow turned to Ula.

"This is where I go on alone," he said.

"Don't try to follow. It's too dangerous. I have the love and trust of my brothers and sisters in the pack, but none of you do."

She gave him a long look, understanding why they had to part. She peered into his eyes without a word. In her eyes, he read sad acceptance that this was it for them. He would never see any of them again, he knew.

He turned to the others. "I'll never forget any of you. Goldie, Switch, I'll always remember you as pack mates. Dog pack mates. But where I will go now, you cannot. I don't fit into the city. I only hope they will remember me and take me back."

They both lowered their heads as a sign of respect to him, and then backed away, giving enough distance for Shadow and Ula to have a moment of privacy.

"I wish I didn't have to go, Ula," Shadow said.

"I wish that, too," Ula replied. "But I understand why you do."

"I will not be boxed into someone's backyard, with my only pack member a fat, indifferent white cat. And I will not be adorned with ribbons tied in my fur by a human child. And I will not eat dried pebbles of dog kibble. Most of all, I will not have a collar around my neck and be jerked around at the end of a strap.

I will not be submissive to humans. No, I will not."

"You could stay. Live on the street with us. Forage for food with us. Protect us. There are only three of us now in the pack. If you stayed, you would be—you must know that you would be my Alpha," she said.

He took in some air. Shadow was not certain he had ever felt more sadness in his heart than he did in that moment, as he feared—no, as he *knew*—that he would never see her again. He knew he could no longer delay and he touched her nose with his, lowering his head.

She pressed her face against his shoulder, and whispered, "Goodbye, Shadow." With that final phrase, she turned and bounded off down the road. Goldie and Switch followed and Shadow turned to walk into the forest alone.

Chapter Fourteen

As Shadow walked toward his home, the familiarity of the trees around him lifted his spirits.

He recognized where he was, in relation to the grove, and decided to go there first. He didn't expect the pack to be there, but it wouldn't hurt to check. Then, he would go even deeper into the forest to see about his favorite escape, the old farm, 'the place of the wall' as his pack mates called it. He took in a deep breath of the clear forest air, a refreshing difference from the acrid, exhaust-laced air of the city.

The sound of the dancing creek met his ears, and he picked up his pace to find the stream.

Once he did, he stopped long enough to have a long, quenching drink. The cool, clear water strengthened his resolve and made him feel a little bit closer to happy. He dunked his head into the water and shook himself dry, the droplets flying away, sparkling in the sun.

The grove was just ahead. He recognized the formation of the trees, but even before he made it to the familiar clearing, he could sense that something was amiss. He neared and saw a strange tape wrapped around some of the trees. He was unsure what they meant, but he could smell the imprint of humans all over the area. He realized that humans had marked some trees in a way that wolves didn't. But their message was clear: They were claiming the trees and he could smell human hands all over them. Some of the smaller trees and underbrush had been cleared away. A strange metal machine stood near the entrance to what was once his den, where he had once slept in warm comfort next to his mother and the other cubs.

A rising panic formed inside his stomach. He circled the area, taking in the impressions he gathered from the smells. Humans had come and would come again. Eventually, they would completely destroy the area. *At least,* he thought with some comfort, *at least I don't sense the smell of death.* Not here, anyway.

So, even though his pack was gone, at least they had been alive when they had last been here. He sniffed around, trying to find one particular scent that seemed to be missing. He tried to explain it away in his mind that she had to be safe, elsewhere.

He was glad they were gone, for their sakes, but sad for his own. For he had come all this way, hoping to be welcomed back into the pack, but they were not even here.

Shadow took off toward the old farm. He didn't know what he would find there, but he had to see with his own eyes what had become of it. When he crested the hill to the place where he used to run and play with ease, he didn't recognize the area. He looked at the trees around him, and knew he was in the correct part of the woods.

However, the place where the rock wall used to be was no longer there. The whole place had the earth turned over and flattened out. The trees that should have been ahead of him had been pulled completely out of the ground and carried away. He wondered what kind of terrible machine had done this. The land had been smoothed over and a large expanse was exposed to the sky. Most of the forest had been completely cleared away. The edge of the clearing also had that strange tape tied around the trunks of the trees. Shadow cowered at the vision before him. The humans had marked their territory everywhere with their tape tied around trees and their smells and their destruction.

The scent of humans and recently used acrid-smelling machines overpowered him, very nearly drowning out the scent of what was one his beloved forest. He heard a movement on the far end of the clearing, and determined right away that another human walked nearby, several of them, by the scents. He didn't know what to do, other than hide in the scant underbrush. But he didn't want to hide. They had taken his home away, after he had spent so much time trying to get back. They had endangered his family. He still didn't know if his pack had all made it to safety.

Shadow darted out of the underbrush, running across the cleared expanse at full speed. As he approached the humans, his anger took over. He began to snarl and bark. This was his territory and they needed to leave right away. He barked with a fierceness as he had never felt before, maybe because he was back in his own territory.

The humans looked surprised and scurried backward. One of them climbed up the side of a heavy machine and the other jumped out of the way of Shadow's bared teeth. He didn't want to bite them, as he imagined the taste of human flesh wouldn't be something he wanted to experience.

But he had already been in one fight today and if it came to that, bite he would. His fur stood out all around him and he spun around, trying to get to both of the humans who evaded him. A male human hand landed on the scruff of his neck. *Not this again.*

As his feet were lifted off the ground, he twisted his body around, his teeth snapping and legs flailing, desperate for escape. He had come too far to be taken by the humans again.

The sound of another dog met his ears. More barking and snarling, not his own. He lost some sense of what was happening when he was dropped back to the dusty ground. He shook his head and turned, only to see Ula, hackles raised and teeth bared, standing at the foot of the human who had grabbed Shadow.

Get to the tree line! she said, sending him a message with her mind.

He didn't hesitate to do so, with her running close at his heels. They didn't stop until they reached the lake at the bottom of the mountains, quite clear of the humans.

"What are you even doing here?" he said, spinning to greet his friend with gratitude and surprise.

"I thought about what Red said," Ula said after catching her breath. "He had once been an Alpha, but he wasn't anymore. I had my time as Alpha. They needed me for that span of time. But leadership was not for me. I left Goldie in charge to start their new pack. There are plenty of dogs in the city. They'll find each other."

"But..." Shadow said.

"Do you want me to go back to them?" Ula asked with a small spark in her eye.

"No!" Shadow insisted. "Of course not!" He caught his excitement and attempted to reel it in. "That is... if you want to come along, you can. If we find the wolves, I just don't know what they'll say about you. We might have to fight."

Ula simply laughed, crinkled her nose and nudged him with her shoulder. "Come on, Shadow. Let's go find your family. That is the first thing. We'll worry about the rest later."

They walked along the side of the lake, both of them stopping to drink from the fresh, cool water, fed by the melted mountain snow. It was the sweetest water that Shadow ever tasted—the taste of home. The pine trees jutted up to the sky, creating a covering of green surrounding them. The air grew cooler as they increased in altitude while climbing the mountains.

He didn't know how long it had been since he had been to the forest. He felt sad that the grove and the old farm had been taken over and changed by the humans. He wondered if there was anyone, anywhere who could stop them. At least, they would be safe up in the steep slopes and in the rocks. They continued walking. Soon, they began to see snow here and there, just in the shade. The sun still had enough warmth to melt the rest of it.

"There's another cave close by," Shadow explained. "Sometimes, they use it during the humans' hunting season. I have never been there, but I have seen it in the mind link of my Alpha."

"Is that what happened to us in the shelter?" Ula asked. "A mind link?"

"I think so," Shadow said. "Before you, I had only ever felt it with the pack. Did you have something like that with Goldie and the others?"

"I think so, but to a small degree," she said. "It's different with you, though. Stronger."

"It is, isn't it?" Shadow said. "I wonder why that is."

"I don't know, but I like it," Ula said.

"So do I."

They walked in silence for a little while. They soon came around the bend to a clearing.

Beyond the clearing, Shadow saw the entrance to the mountain cave. The sun hung low in the sky, but had not yet reached the tree line. He wondered if the pack might be out hunting.

They approached the edge of the clearing, a wide expanse reaching to the cavernous mouth. In the shadows of the cave, he couldn't tell if there was movement, but he walked forward, letting out a short howl. A formal greeting.

Ula waited at the edge of the clearing just opposite the cave. Shadow neared the mouth, emitting another short howl. Still no response. Shadow turned and eyed the edge of the tree line around the clearing. Nothing. He sat down and lifted his nose. Suddenly, a familiar scent greeted his senses.

"Shadow!" Snow's voice rang out across the clearing from the pine trees. He saw her white silhouette bounding out of the shadows. Overcome with joy, he leaped into a full run toward his sister. They met in the middle and pounced on one another, rolling with happiness in a tangle of legs and tails. When they came back to their feet, both laughing and howling and leaping about, he saw that Snow had grown. She now looked like an adult wolf, with broad shoulders and a streamlined bone structure. Her eyes gleamed with a golden hue, much different from the youthful blue they all had the last time they were together.

"Where are the others?" he asked.

"Blue and Chase are hunting, but they'll be back soon. They know, of course, that you are back. We smelled you."

Just as Snow promised, his two brothers appeared side by side, leaping through the pine trees toward their returned long-lost brother. As they approached, Shadow was struck once more by how much they all had matured. Blue had kept the eye color that matched his name, but they both looked like adult wolves. Much like he had greeted Snow, the three leaped, tumbled and rolled in the snowy meadow. Wolfish laughter rang out over the trees. The siblings walked back to the cave, shoulder to shoulder. Shadow noticed that he was the smallest canine there.

"Where are Mother and Alpha?" Shadow asked. "I am very much looking forward to telling everyone about what has happened to me while I was away. And there is something else I would like to tell you all."

A silence fell over the group.

"What has happened?" Shadow asked.

Snow spoke first. "Our numbers have changed since you were with us last. When you disappeared, Mother was in deep mourning. Alpha demanded that anyone who knew anything come forward. No one knew anything, until one day, Cass came to them and confessed that she had seen you go to the place of the wall, the place where the old farm used to be. The forbidden place. The Alpha and Mother were so angry with her for not telling them sooner. Especially with the history between the two of them."

"What history?" Shadow asked. "What are you talking about?"

"To be the Alpha's mate," Snow continued. "A long time ago, before Alpha took over the pack, Cass was trying to catch his eye, to become the Alpha's mate when he ascended. But our father chose Mother over her. I don't think Cass ever got over it. They made peace but never truly became anything other than amicable pack mates, getting along for the sake of keeping the peace."

"I think I remember," Shadow said. "They were never true friends, were they?"

"No," Snow said. "The problem arose as more humans came into the territory. Cass claimed she felt responsible for your absence. She felt that if she had come to the pack when she first found out you had been playing as a puppy at the place by the wall and had seen a human, then we could have all moved up the mountain as we are now."

"She knew?" He digested this information.

"She wanted to try to find you, and despite the Alpha advising strongly against it, she returned to the farm site. She taunted the humans, to the extent that they finally came after her. On that day, though, Mother had gone after her, trying to finally confront her to make peace. Alpha had decided to let another step into his place, and Mother wanted to tell her first before it was announced to the others."

"Father is not the Alpha now?" Shadow was in shock.

"No," Snow said. "He's not."

"I don't understand. What happened?" Shadow asked, but he feared he already knew.

"Our Mother," Snow said somberly. "She was felled by a hunter."

Sadness jolted through him. Suddenly, he understood the power of the sticks that made loud cracking sounds... the guns. "Mother is gone," he said softly, trying to accept the bad news.

"Yes, she is gone. Alpha wanted to move us up the mountain after what happened to her, but Cass remained inconsolable. She insisted that the pack stay in the same place, in case you returned. She wanted to try to clear her conscience, too. It was only days ago that the message came from the bird. The city bird that you sent to tell us to leave."

"You got my message," Shadow said with relief.

"Your message saved our lives. We left the area just as the humans came in and took down the trees with great heavy machines. But..." Snow dropped her eyes, unwilling to go on.

Blue took over the story. "When we came to the mountain cave, Father stepped down as the Alpha. With Mother's death, and your disappearance, all of the Alpha wolf power has gone out of him, he says."

"But... who is the new Alpha?" Shadow asked.

"I am." The voice of Storm came suddenly behind them. Cass stood at his side, but lowered her eyes when Shadow met her with his questioning gaze. Thunder trotted out of the woods and stood on the other side of Storm. The two had always hunted together. Today had been no different.

Shadow realized that Cass had finally gotten her wish. She had found her way to become the Alpha's mate after all. Storm spoke again. "Welcome back, Shadow."

"Thank you." Shadow lowered his head as a show that he recognized Storm as the new Alpha. "May I speak with Cass alone, please?"

Cass stepped forward as the other pack

members stepped back to give them a circle of privacy.

"I am so sorry about your mother," Cass began.

Shadow shook his head to silence her. "I have been among the humans," he said. "Their ways are strange and unpredictable. They don't exist in a way that makes sense to us. I have come to believe that the human that took me thought he was somehow saving me. Likewise, he didn't understand that Mother was not a threat to him. It was not your fault what happened to her, or to me. You are not responsible for any of it."

Cass kept her gaze even until he said this last part. Then, she cast her eyes downward.

"No," said Shadow, lowering his eyes as well. "It is I who must defer to you." He bowed to show his recognition of her as his Alpha female.

She touched him with her nose.

"Thank you," she whispered before stepping back to stand beside Storm.

"There is one more thing." Shadow turned back to the edge of the forest where he knew Ula waited. "I have a guest."

The others turned toward where he looked.

"Actually," Shadow continued, "she's more than a guest. She's coming to stay with us. To join the pack."

"A city dog?" Chase said. "With us?"

"She saved my life. And then, I saved hers. Ula, you can come out now," Shadow called out. The black and white dog stepped out of the shadows. She was nervous in the presence of the wild wolves. However, she bravely stepped forward and now came to stand next to Shadow. "Everyone, this is Ula. She survived the worst imaginable treatment at the hands of humans, who used her to train their most aggressive dogs to fight each other for sport. In self-defense, she had to kill one of them, a much bigger dog, or she would have died. And yesterday, she and I and two other dogs triumphed over a rival pack on the city streets. She was their Alpha and she is worthy of our pack."

There were murmurs of respect for her triumph and bravery.

She lowered her gaze to all of them, and turned her forehead to Storm. "It's nice to meet all of you. I have heard so much about you. Thank you for your kind welcome."

Chase, Snow and Blue all circled her in a greeting, giving her an impromptu once-over. She rolled over on her back to show respect and when they finally let her up, they yipped a welcome. She wagged her tail low and yipped back in a wolf-like way. Shadow was so proud of Ula. So proud. She was very adaptable.

Shadow opened his mind, and allowed them to see Ula as he had seen her earlier that day. The image had flowed into the minds of Shadow's siblings. All at once, they gasped at seeing the fierceness present in the little dog, who was no bigger than their adopted brother. Within seconds, they all expressed a genuine welcome to her.

They all returned to the cave. The pack had brought pieces of the most recent kill back to give to their elderly Father, who had stayed behind. He expressed his happiness at Shadow's return and welcomed him. He smiled when he met Ula and nodded toward Shadow with approval. At last, the pack was together again. And Shadow had a companion who had proven herself in the city and had helped him return to the wilderness.

Storm bumped shoulders with Shadow and said, "Your watch, Little Wolf. That is what we will call you now." And Storm went to the back of the cave out of the wind and lay down with Cass and the others.

It brought him great happiness to be renamed Little Wolf by the new Alpha, and to be entrusted with such an important pack duty as the watch.

As night fell, he lay wide awake in the

clearing, just in front of the cave. He was shocked and sad that Mother Wolf was gone and that Father, now with a muzzle that had gone completely white with age, had given up his Alpha position to Storm. How much time had passed since he had left and returned, he didn't know, but it must have been a long time because now, all of his siblings were adults, as he was. Of course, he was also shocked that the pack had had to leave their home of many generations and migrate to the high country where game was scarcer and they would have to compete for food with bears and cougars.

With the humans and the way they spread themselves far and wide, he knew that it was just a matter of time before the pack would have to find even more remote territory, perhaps even above the tree line, which presented its own problems with longer, harsher winters, less camouflage and even sparser hunting. And perhaps, they might have to fight other migrating wolf packs if their territories overlapped.

Nothing stays the same, he thought. *No matter how much you want it to, it moves with the seasons and becomes something new. Something more challenging.* The only constant was his siblings, but someday, they, too, would give way to the younger ones who would take their places. As would he. And perhaps, he would someday be the one with the white muzzle, waiting for food and for news to be brought to him by one of his offspring. But not too soon, he hoped. He had a lot of catching up to do with the wolf pack. Many hunts to hunt. Many howls to howl.

Alert, he lay with swiveling ears and nostrils pointed into the wind. With Ula sleeping peacefully at his side, Little Wolf watched as, one by one, the stars appeared in the indigo night sky...

The End

About K.T. Tomb:

K.T. Tomb enjoys traveling the world when not writing adventure thrillers. She lives in Portland, OR.

Please find her at: www.kttomb.com

K.T. TOMB

Made in the USA
Middletown, DE
27 June 2023